The Best of Hans Andersen

Illustrated by

Michele Danon-Marcho
and
Maya Filip

English text by
Claire Stewart

Exeter Books

NEW YORK

CONTENTS

English Text Copyright © 1983 by Octopus Books Limited
Illustration Copyright © 1981 by Litor Publishers, Brighton

First published in USA 1985
by Exeter Books
Distributed by Bookthrift
Exeter is a trademark of Simon & Schuster, Inc.
Bookthrift is a registered trademark of Simon & Schuster, Inc.
New York, New York

ISBN 0 671 07541 1

Printed in Czechoslovakia

The Ugly Duckling

It was a glorious summer's day in the country. The cornfields were golden and the hay stood neatly stacked in the green meadows. A mother duck lay on her nest in a deserted spot near an old farm, waiting for her eggs to hatch. The time passed very slowly – especially since no one came to see her. At last, however, the eggs began to crack open and, one by one, the little yellow chicks came blinking into the sunlight.

'Cheep, cheep,' they cried. 'How big the world is!'

'The world is far bigger than this,' said their mother. 'It stretches right across the canal and even beyond the next field, though I have never been there. Now are you all here?' she continued. Then she noticed that one egg, the largest of all, lay still unopened in the nest. With a sigh, she resumed her seat, wondering to herself how much longer. . . .

'Well, how's it going?' asked an old duck who had come to pay her a visit.

'This large egg just won't hatch. But look at the others. Aren't they the prettiest ducklings you ever saw?'

'Let me see the egg that won't hatch,' came the reply. 'Heavens! It looks just like a turkey's egg. Don't waste your time on that one, dear. It will only bring you trouble and, believe me, it will never go near the water. Just teach the other children to swim and leave that one be.'

'Oh, one more day won't hurt me. I think I'll sit it out,' said the resolute mother.

'Well you know best I'm sure,' said the old duck, shaking her head dubiously.

At last, the big egg burst open and out crept a very large, *very* ugly duckling.

The mother duck was worried. 'Can it really be a turkey chick?' she wondered, 'We'll find out for sure tomorrow.'

The next day she took all her chicks down to the water and jumped in. They all followed, one by one, *including* the ugly duckling.

'That's all right then. Now at least I know it isn't a turkey,' said the mother to herself.

She led the chicks into the farmyard to meet their relations, reminding them on the way to keep their toes turned out and look respectful.

But, 'oh no, not *more* new-comers,' was the cry, and one duck, catching sight of the poor little ugly duckling, flew into a disgusted rage, and bit it in the neck.

'It hasn't done you any harm!' cried its mother angrily.

'It's too big and odd-looking and ought to be taught a lesson,' said the rude duck.

'Such a shame. The *others* are so pretty,' remarked the old duck who had visited the nest the day before.

'This one may not be pretty, but it is very well behaved and is the best swimmer of them all. I think he – for it is a drake – will grow up to be very strong. Beauty is not *so* important after all,' said the proud mother.

But the ugly duckling became the laughing stock of the yard. He was jeered at and pecked by the chickens as well as the ducks, while the turkey cock, who was very full of himself, gobbled threateningly at him.

Over the next few days things went from bad to worse. The farmer's daughter kicked him as she fed the poultry and even his brothers and sisters turned against him and wished he would go away.

The ugly duckling was very miserable. Nobody wanted him on the farm, so he decided to go out on to the great moor where the wild ducks lived. The little birds in the bushes flew away when they saw him coming. 'That's because I am so ugly,' thought the duckling sadly, as he settled down alone among the reeds.

Later two wild geese flew by, making fun of the poor outcast as they passed. Suddenly, the duckling heard a loud 'bang, bang', and the two geese fell dead into the water. Hunters lay in wait all over the moor. The blue smoke of gunfire rose from the trees all around and the hunting dogs splashed noisily on every side. The ugly duckling was terrified.

As night fell, the din ceased. So, gathering his courage, the little duckling rose and fled through fields and meadows. A terrible storm raged and, after several hours, he was quite

exhausted. He noticed a strange hut with a door hanging off its hinges. There was just enough space for him to slip inside. Here he found an old woman, a cat and a hen.

As soon as they saw the duckling the cat began to purr, the hen to cluck and the old woman, who had bad eyesight, to cry gleefully:

'What a stroke of luck! A great fat duck! Now we shall have fresh eggs every day. But – suppose it's a drake. Well, we must just wait and see.'

For three weeks she waited . . . but no eggs came . . . One day the cat and the hen, who were accustomed to taking charge of the affairs of the household, questioned the duckling:

'Can you lay eggs?' demanded the hen haughtily.

'No,' replied the bewildered duckling.

'Can you arch your back like this?' challenged the cat.

'No, indeed,' said the poor duckling, almost beside himself with

astonishment. Why could he not do something clever too?

'Then kindly stay in your corner and hold your tongue,' snapped the two together.

Miserably, feeling very dejected the ugly duckling obeyed. But when a breath of fresh air and a ray of sunshine crept through the door, he was seized with such a longing to swim on the water that he fled from the hut out into the wide world.

It was autumn and the leaves were turning brown and falling from the trees. One evening the ugly duckling saw a flock of lovely white birds with long necks flying above him. He admired their beauty and wished he were not so ugly himself.

The winter grew cold and harsh. The hole in which he swam became smaller and smaller as the ice grew thicker and thicker. Finally, worn out by his efforts to prevent it from freezing up altogether, he lay quite still, and was soon fast frozen in the ice.

Early next morning, a farmer saw him, broke the ice and took

the duckling home to his children. They wanted to play with him, but the poor creature got frightened, overturning first a milk churn and then a barrel of flour in his alarm. The farmer's wife screamed angrily at him and he flew away.

Now the ugly duckling noticed that his wings had grown bigger and stronger and that they would carry him easily as far as he wanted to go. One day he found himself in a beautiful sweet-smelling garden. Some elder trees bent their branches down to the water where three glorious swans were enjoying the sunshine. He recognized the magnificent birds and felt again the strange sadness. He flew towards them, crying humbly and piteously, 'Kill me – I am too ugly to share the world with you.'

All at once he caught sight of his reflection in the water. He stopped short in astonishment. What trick was this? For there looking up at him was no hideous, clumsy-looking little bird – but he realized with joy – a beautiful *swan*.

The great swans swam round him, stroking him welcomingly.

Hiding his head under his wings, quite overcome by so much admiration, he thought to himself with a full heart, 'I never even *dreamed* of such happiness when I was still just an ugly duckling!'

The Tinder Box

One day a soldier marching home from the wars – left, right! left, right! – with his knapsack and his bright silver sword, encountered a hideous old witch.

'Good evening, my fine soldier lad,' she said. 'Now if you do as I say you shall have as much money as you could wish – enough to fill that big knapsack of yours.'

'Why . . . er . . . thank you . . .' stammered the astonished soldier.

'Just climb down inside that hollow tree. I'll tie a rope around

you and pull you up when you call,' the old witch told him.

'But what shall I find inside the tree?' asked the soldier.

'Why, money of course!' replied the old witch. 'At the bottom of the tree you will find a great hall lit by three hundred lamps. You will see three doors, each leading to a secret chamber. In the first chamber you will find a great chest. On it will be sitting a dog, with eyes as big as teacups. Don't be afraid, just spread this blue-checked apron on the ground and quickly set the dog on top of it. Then open the chest and take as many copper coins as you like.

'If you prefer silver, you must go on into the second chamber.

There, on another chest, sits a dog with eyes the size of mill wheels. Do exactly as before, and you may have all the silver you desire.

'But if you want gold, you must enter the third chamber. There you will see a third dog, with eyes as big as two round towers. Though he is the fiercest of all, if you set him on my apron he will not harm you and you may fill your sack with gold.'

'That sounds easy enough,' said the soldier. 'But what do you require in return?'

'Just bring me the tinder box my grandmother left down there,' said the old woman mysteriously.

23

So she gave him the apron, tied the rope around his waist and he climbed into the tree.

One after another he encountered the three fearsome dogs, just as the witch had described them. Their huge eyes terrified him, but with the aid of the magic apron he passed each one safely and filled his knapsack with copper, silver and gold.

Finally, he picked up the tinder box and called to the witch to pull him up.

'What are you going to do with this old box?' he asked.

'Mind your own business,' retorted the witch. 'You have your money, isn't that enough?'

'No! I want the tinder box too. Give it to me or I'll kill you.'

When she refused, the soldier cut off her head, pocketed the tinder box and bore his heavy sack into town.

There he lived very grandly, wearing fine clothes and making many new friends.

One day he heard talk of the beauty of the princess.

'How can I get to see her?' he asked.

'You can't,' came the reply. 'She lives in a great walled castle. No one but the cruel old king may go in or out, for it has been prophesied that she will marry a common soldier.'

So the soldier continued his merry life until, one day, he realized that he had only two coins left. Sadly, he moved to a tiny attic room where none of his new friends came to see him.

One very dark evening, the soldier remembered the tinder box. No sooner had he struck a light than – lo and behold – there was the dog with eyes as big as teacups!

'What is your command master?' asked the dog.

Then the soldier understood the secret of the witch's tinder box. Now he could have anything he desired. The dog brought him a bag of silver and he became rich and popular once more.

One night, as he lay in bed thinking of the beautiful princess, the soldier had an idea. Summoning the dog with eyes as big as teacups, he told him to bring the princess to him.

In the morning, the princess told her parents of what she thought had been a strange dream. The following morning the same thing happened, and the morning after that and the morning after that . . . The old king was suspicious, but in spite of all his attempts, he could not discover where the princess disappeared to every night. But the queen had a plan. She hid a bag of grain with a hole in it in the princess's clothing. So that night a trail was left which led right to the soldier's door. He was arrested and condemned to death.

Thousands of people came to see the execution. The king and queen looked on from their splendid thrones. When the guards brought in the poor soldier, he made a last request; to smoke a final pipe. The king agreed, so he took out the magic tinder box and struck it – one, two, three – and at once there stood all three dogs, their great eyes glaring furiously.

They immediately attacked and killed the king and queen. A great cheer went up from the crowd, who hated the old rulers.

'Long live the brave soldier! He shall be king!' they cried.

So the princess and the soldier were married. It was the most magnificent wedding ever seen and the three dogs, who sat at the great table, opened their huge eyes wider than ever.

The Little Mermaid

In the deepest depths of the ocean, where the strangest plants and flowers grow and all different types of fish live, lies the castle of the Merking.

Its walls are made of coral, its windows of clearest amber. Its roof is tiled with shells and in each shell lies a beautiful white pearl of priceless value.

Now the Merking had six little daughters and, being a widower, he had entrusted their education to his old mother, a clever and proud lady who, as a sign of her high rank, always wore twelve oysters on her tail. She loved the children dearly and cared for them strictly, but kindly, and her grand-daughter loved her too.

All the princesses were beautiful, but the youngest was the loveliest of all. Her skin was as clear and smooth as pure silk, her eyes blue as the deepest sea, and her beautiful tail as graceful and shimmering as water itself.

The Merking had given each of his daughters her own little garden to do with as she wished. While all the others made grand displays of the beautiful things they had been given from the wrecks of ancient ships, the youngest would have nothing but a small marble statue of a young boy.

She was a quiet, thoughtful child and loved nothing better than to hear her grandmother talk of the world of dry land that existed above them. This strange place, where the flowers all had beautiful fragrances and the fishes (called birds by the land people) sang among the great plants called trees, haunted the little mermaid's dreams. She longed for her fifteenth birthday when, according to mer-custom, she would be allowed to visit the surface of the ocean and sit on the rocks to watch the great ships sailing by.

When the eldest princess was fifteen, she rose to the surface and, on her return, reported to her sisters what she had seen and heard: the noise of people talking and laughing, the sound of church bells and the sight of lights twinkling on the shore.

The youngest little mermaid listened with shining eyes. Now, whenever she stood at the open window and looked up through the dark blue water, she thought of the bustling city, and of the strange creatures her grandmother had described who could move as easily on land as she could herself in the sea.

The second sister came to be fifteen and when she returned she described the sun setting amidst a bank of clouds. When it was the third princess's turn, she saw the green of hills topped with castles and palaces, while the fourth preferred to stay far out at sea and watch the great tall-masted ships, the whales and the dolphins. The fifth princess's birthday fell during the winter and so she saw a different scene. The sea was quite green and great icebergs floated by, moulded into strange shapes and sparkling like diamonds.

At last the day the little mermaid had longed for arrived. She too was fifteen! With a brief cry of farewell, she rose, light and clear as a water bubble, up and up through the depths of the sea. Just as the sun was setting her little head, crowned with a wreath of white lilies (but each lily was really half a pearl), appeared above the surface.

The air was fresh and warm on her face. Quite close to her the little mer-

maid saw a great ship with three tall masts. There was music and singing on board and, as the night grew darker, hundreds of coloured lanterns were lit. The little mermaid looked on enchanted.

The little mermaid could see many sailors on the ship, but the most handsome of all, a young prince, stood on the bridge, richly dressed and smiling. It was his birthday and all his companions were cheering and drinking his health.

Although it was getting late, the little mermaid could not bear to leave this delightful spectacle or to stop staring at the handsome young prince. All at once, the waves began to rise higher, great clouds appeared and forks of lightning flashed. Taken by surprise, the sailors hurried to furl the sails. But they

were too late. The great ship was lashed by cruel seas – one moment disappearing into a valley of water, next re-emerging tossed on a mountainous crest of foam. With a great crack, the ship's timbers broke, the tall masts snapped in two like reeds, and suddenly it sank beneath the heaving ocean.

As the ship broke up, the little mermaid saw the prince disappearing into the sea. For a moment she was happy, thinking that now he would come down and live with her in her father's palace. Then she remembered that land people could not live in the water without air to breathe. The prince was in mortal danger!

At once, without a thought for her own safety, she dived among the crashing waves and splintered planks of the wreck to save the drowning young man. Holding his head tenderly above the surface, she rested, allowing the waves to carry them.

35

By morning the storm was over and there was not a sign of the ship. It was as if nothing had happened. But the prince still lay motionless in the water beside her, his eyes closed, so the little mermaid knew that it had not been all a dream. As she looked at him, it seemed to her that he was very like the little marble statue in her garden at home. Gently she kissed his noble forehead, wishing with all her heart that he might live.

After a while she came upon a calm bay where a rock and some white sand had been cast up to make a pleasant beach. Quickly she swam towards the shore. Laying the prince on the sand with his head raised towards the life-giving warmth of the sun, she returned to the safety of the waves, hiding behind a rock to observe what might happen.

A young girl came running across the beach and bent over the prone figure. Then the little mermaid saw with delight that the prince stirred, looked up and smiled at the girl. Hurrying away towards the nearby town, the girl soon returned with a crowd of helpers, who carefully carried the prince away.

Although she was very happy to see that the prince was alive, the little mermaid felt very sad as he disappeared from her sight – perhaps for ever.

When she returned to her home, the other mermaids all asked her what she had seen. But the melancholy little mermaid would tell them nothing. Many, many times she returned to the place where she had left the prince, hoping for a glimpse of his handsome face, but he was never to be seen.

Her only comfort was to sit in her garden and look wistfully at the little statue that reminded her of her dear prince. She would sit and weep, singing softly to herself in a voice of such sweetness and clarity that even the fish stopped to listen.

At last, when she could bear her sorrow no longer, she told her

grandmother the whole story. Alas, the old lady agreed that there was nothing to be done – unless . . .

There was a sea witch – a terrifying old sorceress – whose help, for those who dared ask it, was very powerful.

The young mermaid was determined to seek her help and swam through roaring whirlpools and past monstrous slimy creatures to find her. Whenever fear told her to turn back, she recalled the face of the handsome prince and continued on her way.

At last she came upon the old crone, seated in front of her house of bleached sailors' bones. She seemed to be waiting for her.

'I know what it is you desire,' said the sea witch. 'You want to exchange your tail for two legs so that the young prince may fall in love with you. Very well, I will prepare you a potion, but,' here the old witch grinned evilly, 'there is a price to pay. You must give me that sweet singing voice of yours and if the man you love

should marry another, you will die. Whatever happens, you may never return to your home beneath the waves. And every step you take on your pretty new legs will be like treading on sharp knives. Are you still so sure this is what you want?'

'I am sure,' said the little mermaid.

Having looked for the last time on her father's castle, she turned and sped away to the bay where she had left the prince. As soon as she was near land she drank the witch's potion. Immediately a pain passed through her so sharp that she fainted and collapsed. When she awoke, there stood her beloved prince.

She tried to speak but found that she could not. Then she remembered the witch's bargain and, looking down, she saw that her tail had been transformed into the prettiest little white legs.

The prince took her to his court. All who saw her admired the sad beauty of her face and the natural grace of her movements. For the prince's pleasure she danced and danced, though every

step was as painful as treading on red hot steel. The prince called her 'his little sea-orphan' and grew to love her like his own sister.

One day he confided to the little mermaid, that ever since the day of the great storm, his heart had been haunted by the face of the young girl who had first summoned help for him. The prince did not understand the reason for the heartfelt sigh with which his companion received this news. And she could never tell him . . .

The prince was invited to visit a nearby kingdom. With the little mermaid ever faithful at his side, he travelled across the sea. He was overjoyed when he recognized the foreign king's daughter as the very girl whom he had loved for so long. She too recognized the prince, and soon they were married.

As the wedding guests danced among the coloured lanterns on the prince's ship – so like the scene of her first sight of him – the little mermaid wept bitterly. For she knew that, by the witch's decree, she must soon die. Still she danced along with the rest and the agonizing pain in her feet was as nothing to the pain of her breaking heart.

When all was at last quiet on board, the little mermaid stood waiting for the dawn which would, she knew, bring her death. Then suddenly she saw her sisters rising from the ocean.

'We have sold our beautiful long hair to the sea witch,' they told her. 'In return she gave us this knife. If you plunge it into the prince's heart and let his blood fall on your feet, you will become a mermaid again and can return with us beneath the sea. Hurry!'

But, with a shake of her head and a look of infinite sadness at the prince as he lay sleeping, the little mermaid flung the cruel knife – and then herself – into the waves.

She felt her body dissolving into foam . . . then all at once she began to rise; lighter than air, she was lifted towards the sky.

She saw the bright sun and over her head sailed hundreds of

glorious, ethereal beings – she could see them through the red clouds in the sky. Their speech was melody, but no human ear could hear their song and no human eye could see them. Without wings they floated through the air.

'Where am I going?' she asked.

'To live with us,' said one of the beings.

The daughters of the air, for so these creatures were, had taken pity on the innocent, loving creature. Henceforth, she would live with them for ever, remaining eternally faithful in her watch over the prince and his beloved, their children and *their* children.

The Fir Tree

Once upon a time in a great forest a little fir tree grew, surrounded by many larger friends and relations. When children passed by on their way to school, they often called out to each other:

'Look at that pretty little one! Isn't it lovely?'

But the little fir tree took no notice, only sighing to himself:

'Oh if only I were a great big tree like the others! Then I would spread my branches wide to look out over the whole world and the birds would build their nests in my boughs. I am so tiny that in winter hares come and play leapfrog over my head – it makes me *very* cross!' And his little branches shook and rustled angrily.

The little fir tree was so unhappy that he no longer enjoyed the warmth of the sunshine, the singing of the birds, or watching the clouds sail across the sky.

Two winters went by, and by the third the fir tree had grown so tall that the cheeky hares were forced to abandon their old game and run round him.

Every autumn woodcutters came to the forest and cut down a few of the largest trees. Now that he too was grown up, the fir tree trembled with fear like the others at the sound of the great saws.

When the noble trees fell to the ground, their branches were cut off so that they looked quite different, naked. Then they were loaded on to wagons and towed away. The fir tree often wondered where they went and what became of them.

In the spring, when the swallows and storks came, the fir tree asked them if they knew the answer.

'Yes, I know,' said a fatherly old stork. 'On my way here from Egypt I flew over the sea. There I saw many ships with huge tall masts. I believe those were once trees – and they smelt like firs. They're very impressive I can tell you.'

What kind of thing is the sea? What does it look like?' asked the fir tree excitedly.

But the old stork was in too much of a hurry to explain.

'Enjoy your freedom while you can,' advised the sunshine.

And the wind kissed the tree and the dew shed crystal tears on him; but the young tree did not understand what they meant. He thought only of the world of excitement and adventure beyond the forest.

At Christmas-time, many of the most attractive young trees were felled and carried away. Their boughs, however, were not trimmed.

'Where do they go? Why do they keep their branches?' asked the fir tree.

'We know! We know!' chirped the sparrows. 'We have looked through the windows of houses in the town and seen them planted in the middle of the room. They are decorated with all sorts of beautiful things.'

'That sounds even better than sailing on the sea,' cried the young fir tree. 'How I long to be one of them! Perhaps it will be my turn next year.'

'Be content to stay here with us,' said the gentle breeze as it brushed softly through his branches.

But the tree was not at all happy, and did not hear the good

advice that was being given to him.

Winter and summer the fir tree grew, until it was one of the finest in the whole forest. Finally, one Christmas, it was cut down.

How strange, that as it fell, the fir tree felt none of the happiness and excitement he had dreamed of for so long, but only pain and a sensation of faintness. With a shock he realized that he was sad to leave his home and friends forever.

When he awoke, the tree was being unloaded in a great courtyard. A voice said:

'That one's lovely; I'll take that one.'

Two liveried footmen came and carried him away. He was placed in a beautiful drawing room among painted vases and richly covered furniture. The servants planted him in a tub and began to decorate him with sweets and coloured balls. Then they hung his branches with a hundred little candles, red, white and blue and fastened a splendid tinsel star at the top. It was the proudest and happiest moment of the fir tree's life!

'How I wish it were evening, so that the candles could be lit. I wonder if the sparrows will come and look in at me through the window.'

At last it grew dark, the room began to fill with people, and the candles were lighted. What a wonderful sight! The fir tree trembled so much at his own splendour that one of the candles fell and set light to a twig. With cries of alarm, two servants flew to put out the little flame.

As the people laughed and talked, the rest of the candles burned down and the fir tree did his very best to stand stock still so that there would be no more accidents. His back began to ache most dreadfully from the effort, but he did not care, for this was his moment of glory.

Finally, when the last candle had been extinguished, the

children who were gathered at the far end of the room rushed forward to collect their presents. They fell upon the poor fir tree so roughly that several of his branches were cracked and, if he had not been securely fastened, he would surely have fallen. He was a little alarmed by this treatment and by all the unaccustomed noise, glitter and gaiety.

Clutching their new toys in their arms, the children danced about the tree. But their thoughts were no longer for him. Now they were shouting for a new diversion:

'A story! Tell us a story!' they cried, and they dragged a little fat man towards the tree. He gathered all the children about him and began:

'This is the story of Clumpy-Dumpy, who fell down the stairs, but picked himself up to marry a princess and become a king.'

And the little man told the story and the children laughed and clapped their hands, before returning to play with their new toys.

All that night the fir tree stood deep in thought. For he too had listened to the story of Clumpy-Dumpy, but he had *believed* it. He felt how wonderful the world must be in which such fine things could happen. Perhaps he too would one day marry a beautiful princess, for surely he was splendid enough!

In the morning, when the servants entered the drawing-room, he thought to himself, 'Now it will all begin again.' But, instead of decking him with finery, they dragged him roughly from the room and upstairs to a dim and musty attic and locked the door.

The fir tree was puzzled – and just a little frightened. Then he thought again and smiled, saying out loud:

'I know. It's winter outside and the ground is hard and unyielding. The kind people are sheltering me here till the spring comes. Only . . .' And he looked around the empty room with a small sigh – 'it is terribly lonely up here.'

50

'Eek! Eek!' came a little voice, as if from nowhere. It was a little mouse who was shortly followed by his entire family, until the fir tree was surrounded by the tiny inquisitive creatures. They asked him many questions and the tree was very glad to tell them about the days of his youth in the old forest. He told the wondering mice of the beauty of the flowers and the songs of the birds and even smiled as he recalled the hares that used to jump over his head. How happy that time seemed to him now – and how long ago.

Then one morning some servants came and rummaged in the attic. Seeing the tree leaning against the wall, they dragged it out and down the stairs until it felt again the fresh air and the warm sunshine in its branches.

'Now, my life is beginning again,' he thought, looking around. Everything in the garden was in bloom. Roses hung, fresh and fragrant, over the little fence, lime trees were flowering and birds sang with all their might.

Joyfully the fir tree spread his branches wide. It was only then that he noticed how withered and yellow they had become and how he lay in a neglected corner of the garden among a clump of nettles and weeds. Only the tinsel star that remained fastened to his topmost branch reminded him of his former splendour.

After a while, a servant came over and examined the old tree. Taking a small axe, he chopped the tree into little pieces and gathered them into a great bundle.

Blazing brightly in the grate, the fir tree sighed deeply. Each sigh sounded like the crack of a whip and made the children who

were playing nearby laugh and cry out, 'bang! bang!' But with each explosion, which was really a sigh, the fir tree thought of a summer day in the forest, or a winter night there when the stars shone brightly. He thought of Christmas Eve and of the story of Clumpy-Dumpy.

When one of the children stooped and picked up the tinsel star and pinned it to his shirt, the fir tree's last souvenir of his happiest evening was gone. With a last sigh and a whiff of sweet-smelling smoke, the tree's life came to an end. And now this story too is ended – and that's the way of all stories.

The Little Tin Soldier

Once upon a time there were twenty-five tin soldiers. They all lived together in a big box, and the first sound they heard in the world was the excited voice of a little boy, as he opened the lid to let them out;

'Tin soldiers!' he cried, and clapped his hands.

It was the little boy's birthday. Carefully he unwrapped the soldiers one by one and set them on the table. Their uniform was red and blue and each one carried a shining musket across his shoulder. They looked very splendid.

When the little boy came to the last tin soldier in the box, he stopped, puzzled. For although it stood as upright and smart as the rest, this little figure had only one leg. This is the story of that one very remarkable tin soldier.

Of all the toys that stood on the table in the little boy's room,

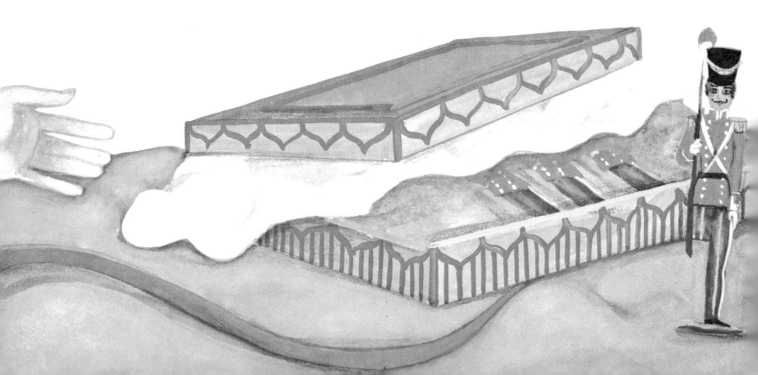

the most impressive was a tall castle made out of pink cardboard. It had high, pointed towers and iron gates and in front of it some little trees were placed round a tiny mirror to represent a lake. Swans made out of wax swam on the shining surface and their reflection was magical and pretty. But prettiest of all was a little paper girl who stood at the open door of the castle. Her dress was made of silvery gauze and a narrow blue ribbon hung over her shoulders, attached to which was a beautiful shining tinsel rose. The girl held out both her arms gracefully, for she was a dancer. To the little tin soldier, she appeared the most beautiful creature in the world. When she raised one leg so high above her head that he lost sight of it, he thought that she, like him, had only one leg. Surely they were made for each other!

But when he remembered that he had only the box to offer her as a home, the little tin soldier thought to himself sadly:

'That is no place for her. She is so grand and beautiful and lives in a great castle, while I am only a common soldier. How can I ever hope to meet her?'

Lying full length hidden behind a snuff box, he watched the little paper girl for many hours, silently admiring her pretty face and the way she continued to stand on one leg without losing her balance.

When evening came, all the other tin soldiers were put back

into their box and the people in the house went to bed. As soon as silence fell, the toys began to play. The puppets turned somersaults and the clockwork canary began to sing sweetly, so that the others could dance to its music.

Only the little tin soldier and the paper dancer remained motionless. She stood elegantly on the very point of one of her toes and he gazed and gazed at her. . . .

Suddenly the clock struck twelve and the lid flew off the snuff box. A little black goblin stared ferociously at the little tin soldier.

'Now then, what do you think you're staring at?' it said.

But the soldier pretended not to hear him.

'Just you wait till tomorrow!' snapped the goblin.

When morning came and the little boy returned to his room, he put the little tin soldier by the window to keep watch.

Suddenly – and whether it was a gust of wind or the wicked little goblin that did it we shall never know – the window flew open and the little soldier fell head first into the street below.

With his one leg pointing helplessly towards the sky and his bayonet pinned between two paving stones he lay, unable to move, in the gutter.

When the little boy rushed into the street to search for his one-legged toy, his foot passed within inches of the little tin soldier's head. But the child did not see him and finally gave up in despair and returned to the house. The soldier was quite alone.

Then it began to rain, at first just a few drops and then harder and harder, until it was coming down in torrents. When it finally stopped, two boys caught sight of the little tin soldier:

'Look! What fun!' they cried. 'Let's make a boat and send the soldier on a campaign across the sea.'

So they made a boat out of newspaper and stood the little tin soldier in the middle of it. Then they pushed it off down the gutter. The waves rose high around the little boat and the current ran faster and faster, for the rain had turned the gutter into a river of dirty churning water. Rocked and buffeted by the water, the tin soldier trembled; but he stood firm, his expression never changed, and he looked straight ahead, with his musket on his shoulder.

All at once the boat entered a long drain and it became as black as night. A great water rat loomed up out of the darkness:

'Stop! Tell me who you are and where you've come from,' it said fiercely.

The tin soldier was silent, gripping his musket more tightly than ever, and the boat sailed on. The furious rat pursued it for as long as it could, gnashing its great teeth and calling out:

'Stop him! Stop him! He hasn't declared himself.'

The current was getting stronger, carrying the little tin soldier further and further from his home and from his beloved paper lady. A roaring sound grew loud in his ears and suddenly he saw that the drain opened into a great canal.

He was already so near that he could not stop. The boat flew

over the edge. The little tin soldier stiffened himself for the fall – and no one observing would have seen him flinch in the slightest. The boat whirled round and round and filled right to the brim with water. The tin soldier stood up to his neck and the boat sank deeper and deeper until at last the waves closed over his head.

At that very moment he was swallowed up by a great fish.

What seemed like a long time later something flashed like lightning, and a voice cried: 'Why, it's the tin soldier!'

The fish had been caught and carried to market. There it had been purchased and taken into the kitchen of the very same house from which the little tin soldier had been lost. The cook had cut it open with a big knife and come upon the one-legged hero.

At first the little boy seemed delighted to have found his old toy again and put him in pride of place on the old table where, at last, he saw again the graceful and well-remembered figure of the paper dancer.

Then one day, the little boy noticed how tarnished and rusty his old toy had become. Whether the child decided he was too ugly to remain on the table or whether the wicked old goblin was still working his evil magic no one will ever know, but suddenly the little tin soldier was hurled into the fire.

He stood in the heart of the flames, still proudly at attention, and felt the terrible heat melt him to the very heart. He looked at the pretty dancer and she looked at him. He knew that he was melting fast, but still he stood firm and upright. Then suddenly the window flew open, a gust of wind caught the dancer and she flew into the fire next to the little tin soldier.

When someone came in the morning to empty the grate, nothing remained of the two faithful toys but a tiny piece of tin in the shape of a heart and on it the dancer's tinsel rose, now burned as black as coal.

The Flying Trunk

There was once a rich merchant's son. When his father died, the young man inherited all his money – enough to pave the streets of the whole town with gold.

However, the son was not as wise as his father had been and he lived so extravagantly, even making paper darts out of bank notes and playing ducks and drakes on the beach with gold coins instead of pebbles, that it was not too long before he had only a few coppers left.

One day a friend sent him an old trunk in which to pack up his possessions, for he had to leave his house and seek his fortune elsewhere. It was all very well, but the young man had nothing left to pack, his only clothes being the pair of slippers and dressing gown in which he was dressed.

So he sat down despairingly on the old trunk to consider his fate. But when he accidentally touched the lock, the trunk sprang

suddenly open and the astonished youth found himself gathered up and flying through the air – up through the chimney and over the clouds, further and further from the scene of his troubles. This was obviously no ordinary trunk. . . .

After some time the trunk was flying over Turkey. Here it appeared to decide that it had gone far enough, for, circling gracefully, it swooped earthwards and finally came to rest in a forest. Hiding his magic trunk under some dry leaves, the merchant's son made his way to the nearest town.

He found he passed unnoticed among the local people, for they too were dressed like him, in dressing gowns and slippers. As he walked about, the young man was puzzled by the sight of a great tower which stood on a hill overlooking the town. Its windows were cut so high into the stone that not even a bird could have seen inside. The young man enquired eagerly why this should be and who lived there.

'The sultan's beautiful daughter,' he was told. 'It is prophesied, you know, that she will be made very unhappy by a lover – so the sultan and sultana do not allow anyone to visit her.'

'The poor girl,' thought the merchant's son to himself. 'How lonely she must be.'

He hurried back to the forest, found the trunk and, as if it read his mind and also knew the way to the great tower, it flew directly to where the princess lived. It landed on the roof and the young man crept silently through the high window into the princess's room.

There she lay, asleep on a sofa. She was so beautiful that the youth's heart was immediately captured and he gently kissed her. The princess woke up with a startled cry and stared wonderingly at the stranger who stood before her. Where had he come from? And *how*?

The merchant's son told her that he was a Turkish angel who had seen her lonely life and come down to visit out of pity because she was so young and fair. The princess's big eyes opened wide with delight and she listened with growing admiration as the youth invented wonderful stories of life above the stars. By the end, it was hard to say which of the two was the more bewitched, so that when the merchant's son asked her if she would marry him, the young princess answered 'yes' at once.

'But you must come to tea on Saturday and meet my mother and father. I am sure they will be proud for me to marry a Turkish angel, but you must tell them one of your very best stories to win their trust as you have won my love. My mother likes stories with a moral, but my father likes to be amused.'

As a token of her love, the princess gave him a sword encrusted with gold coins. He could give her nothing but the promise of his love and the story he would tell on Saturday.

He returned to the wood, sat on the old trunk and worked very hard to make up his story. It was very difficult, for he had used all

his best tales to woo the princess, and this one must be even better – the most important story of his life.

On Saturday he used one of the coins from the sword to buy himself a new dressing gown. When he attended the court, the princess, the sultan and the sultana made him very welcome. They settled him on a great cushion with his tea and prepared to listen to his story:

'In the kitchen of a great mansion, some matches were boasting of their high birth and the wealth of their ancestors. Then all the utensils began arguing as to which of them was truly the grandest and most important. Each insisted it was more nobly descended or more valuable than its neighbour.

First the pot told a long story of the aristocratic grandeur of its youth on the Baltic shore and was awarded a dusty wreath of discarded parsley by the cheeky broom. Then the tongs boldly performed an elegant dance and they too demanded a parsley garland.

At this point the tea urn said that she would have sung for them all, but she was only used to performing in really grand parlours. The kettle burst out angrily that anyway he was the singer in this kitchen and the tea urn merely an affected foreigner. It would be unpatriotic to compare her paltry talents with his own. He asked the shopping basket to judge the issue. At this point the quill pen (who thought himself of superior education) splashed a spot of ink in disgust.

But the shopping basket sniffed disapprovingly, as if such trivial matters were far beneath her dignity, and began to order everyone about in order to restore tidiness to "this *ghastly* mess". At this, all the utensils once again broke out into arguments. The noise was deafening!

All this time, however, the matches looked on without saying a word, for they were perfectly sure that they were the most important. The others were only common tools after all.

Just at that moment a little girl came in and everything in the room became motionless. Without a moment's hesitation, she took the matches and lit the fire with them. They sputtered dramatically and burst into flames. "Now at last," they thought, "everyone can see that we are the grandest. Look how we shine! See how brightly we . . ." The girl had blown them out.'

The sultan and the sultana were both very pleased with the story, and the princess clapped her hands and looked at the merchant's son with shining eyes.

As the wedding day approached, the young man racked his brains to think of an exciting wedding gift. Then an idea came to him. He bought an enormous collection of fireworks, and climbing into the magic trunk, rose high into the air and circled the town. As he went he set off an array of coloured rockets and crackers that exploded right across the sky. Then all the people were convinced that it was indeed a Turkish angel who was to marry their princess.

What tales people tell! When he returned to the town, he overheard people explaining what they had seen!

'I saw the Turkish angel himself,' said one. 'He had eyes like glowing stars and a beard like foaming water.'

'He flew in a cloak made out of pure fire,' cried another.

The merchant's son laughed and laughed. He was very happy, for the following day he was to be married.

That night he returned to the forest to sleep for the last time in his magic flying trunk. But when he came to the place where he had left it, it was nowhere to be seen.

Then with horror he realized the answer to the mystery. A smouldering paper from one of the fireworks had fallen down inside the trunk and set it alight.

Now he could no longer fly. He could no longer be the Turkish angel. He could never claim a princess as his bride.

The princess stood on the roof all day long waiting for her beloved – probably she is waiting still for the Turkish angel who flew down from the sky and into her heart. As for the young man, he wanders through the world, telling stories to earn his living.

Little Ida's Flowers

Little Ida had a great friend. He was a young student, very clever, and very kind. He told her wonderful stories and cut pretty little paper dolls for her. Little Ida was very fond of him.

So one day, when she found that her favourite flowers were withered and dying, Ida consulted the student.

'They were so pretty yesterday,' she said, the tears welling in her eyes. 'Why did it happen?'

'Oh, that's nothing to worry about,' cried the student, laughing. 'Those flowers were at a dance last night. That's what's the matter with them.'

'But flowers can't dance!' exclaimed Ida.

'Oh yes they can, you know. They wait until it's dark and we are all asleep and then they begin. They have a dance almost every night.'

'But where do they dance?'

'You've seen the great castle where the king lives in summer, where you go sometimes to feed the lovely white swans? Well, that's where the best dances are held.'

'But when I was there yesterday, I didn't see a single flower and all the trees were bare. Where have all the flowers gone to? I saw so many in the summer.'

'They're inside the castle,' replied the student. 'For, as soon as the king departs for the town, the flowers all run out of the garden and into the castle. Then they have a really good time. The two most beautiful roses sit on the thrones as king and queen. All the foxgloves stand on either side in long rows and bow and curtsey, and the prettiest of the young flowers dance to entertain the royal

roses. The blue violets, dressed like naval cadets, waltz gracefully with the young lady hyacinths, while the tulips and tiger lilies look on like old ladies to see that the young flowers behave themselves.'

'Doesn't anyone mind the flowers being there?' asked little Ida.

'Nobody really knows about it,' answered the student. 'For when the keeper goes on his rounds at night, the flowers hear his keys rattling long before he arrives, and they are very quiet and hide behind the long curtains.'

'How wonderful!' cried little Ida, clapping her hands.

'If you peep in through the window next time you go into the castle garden, you will see them. That's what I did today.'

'But what about the flowers from the botanical garden? Surely it's too far for them to travel?' asked Ida.

'Ah, but they can fly there. Haven't you seen the lovely red, white and yellow butterflies in your garden? They look almost like flowers sometimes; and that is what they once were. When there is to be a dance at the castle each gentleman flower will invite his lady to go.'

'The flowers talk to each other?' exclaimed Ida, quite astonished.

'Not with words like us certainly, but with signs,' replied the student. 'Haven't you noticed that when there is a breeze the flowers nod at one another and move their leaves? They can understand their movements just as easily as we can when we speak to each other.'

'You are very clever to know all this,' said little Ida, smiling admiringly.

At that moment a nosy old man who had come to visit Ida's family passed by and exclaimed grumpily, 'You shouldn't tell such idiotic tales to a young child. Good heavens, man, she might

80

believe you! Talking and dancing flowers, indeed! Nonsense!'

This crusty old gentleman had taken a dislike to the young student when he had cut out a paper figure of an old witch riding on a broomstick with her husband balanced on her nose. This he thought a joke in very poor taste.

But little Ida thought deeply about what the student had told her, and that evening she laid her withered flowers in her doll's bed – much to the doll, Sophie's annoyance, for now she had to sleep in a drawer – thinking that a good night's sleep might revive them.

When she was about to go to bed herself, she peeped behind the curtain where her mother's beautiful flowers stood in pots on the window sill.

'I know you're going to the dance tonight!' she whispered.

But the flowers pretended not to hear and did not stir a single leaf.

That night, Ida lay awake for some time thinking what a pretty sight it must be to see the flowers dancing in the king's castle.

'I wonder if my flowers really did go there last night,' she thought as she fell asleep.

In the middle of the night, she woke again. What was it that had aroused her? Raising her head, she listened, and it seemed to her she heard someone playing the piano in the next room. The flowers!

She crept silently out of her little bed and stole to the door of the next room. When she looked in, what a wonderful sight met her eyes!

At the piano sat a great yellow lily, swaying to the beautiful airy notes of the music. Her mother's flowers stood in two long rows in the centre of the room; all the pots in the window were empty. On the floor flowers were circling gracefully, holding each other lightly by their long green leaves. No one noticed little Ida as she looked on in wonder and delight.

Just at that moment there was a loud knocking from the drawer where Ida's doll, Sophie, was lying. The old chimney sweep doll, who had been dancing with the flowers, hurried to let her out. She was very impatient and did not even wait for an invitation to join the dancing. Ida was quite ashamed of her doll's bad manners. But the flowers whose bed Sophie had provided greeted her most kindly, complimenting her on her pretty straw hat and dress of delicate pink. Sophie was so pleased that she told the flowers they might keep her bed.

'Thank you very much,' they responded. 'But we cannot live long and tomorrow we shall be quite withered. But please tell your kind little mistress, Ida, that she must not mind, for if she quickly puts us out in the garden, we shall wake up again in the summer and be far more beautiful.'

Sophie promised to convey the message and little Ida gasped as the door opened and a host of splendid flowers entered. These must be the ones from the castle – the ones the student had told her about, for at the head of the procession were two glorious roses, each with a little gold crown. Carnations and pinks followed in courtly rows and also little white snowdrops which tinkled just like bells as they moved.

The flowers danced and danced until the moon began to sink and the faintest glow of dawn stole through the window. At last they all wished one another goodnight and little Ida, too, crept back to her bed and dreamed of all the wonders she had seen.

As soon as she woke, Ida hurried to look at the flowers she had left in Sophie's bed. Sure enough, as they had said, they were quite dead. Ida looked expectantly at her doll, where she lay, still sleeping, in the drawer. But Sophie said nothing.

'You naughty doll,' said Ida. 'Have you forgotten your promise? For that, you shall go on sleeping in that nasty drawer.'

Then she took a small coloured box covered in paintings of

beautiful birds and carefully laid the dead flowers in it.

'There! That will make a pretty coffin for you. And when my cousins come to visit me later on I will ask them to help me bury you in the garden, so that you will grow again in the summer and be more beautiful than ever.'

The cousins were two merry boys. Their names were Gustave and Adolphe. Their father had given them two new crossbows, and they had brought these with them to show Ida. She told them both about the poor flowers which had died and asked them if they would help her to bury them. She showed them the pretty box and the boys agreed.

'Why don't we do it very properly?' said Gustave. 'When Great-grandmother died, the mason made a beautiful cross.'

The two boys went into the garden and found two pieces of wood which they tied together to make a cross.

The next morning the three children descended to the garden in a slow procession. In front went the two boys, who had brought their bows with them and held them across their shoulders like rifles. Behind them came little Ida, carrying the box, and looking very solemn.

When she had placed the box in the little hole that the cousins had dug, and they had carefully replaced the earth and marked the spot with the wooden cross, little Ida murmured tenderly:

'Sleep well, little flowers. Come back soon and fill my garden with scent and colour.'

Then Adolphe and Gustave fired a salvo of arrows over the tiny grave with as much pride and grandeur as at any royal funeral.

'Thank you,' said Ida.

And they all three ran off back through the silent garden towards the house.

Old Shut-Eye's Visits to Hjalmaar

At night, when children are asleep, Old Shut-Eye comes and sits at the head of their beds. His coat is made of silk and under his arm, whatever the weather, he carries an umbrella. Sometimes it has beautiful coloured pictures on it and he often opens it over the heads of the good children, so that they dream the most wonderful stories all night long. Sometimes, however, the umbrella is only an ordinary dull black colour. This is reserved for the naughty children, who sleep heavily and dream of nothing at all.

Nobody in the whole world knows such wonderful stories as Old Shut-Eye. But that you may judge for yourself. . . .

Every evening for one week Old Shut-Eye visited a little boy called Hjalmaar, and each night he created for him a wonderful

story to dream while he slept.

On Monday, as soon as Hjalmaar was asleep, Shut-Eye changed all the flower pots into great trees which spread their branches right across the ceiling. All the twigs bore flowers more beautiful than the loveliest summer rose and soon the whole room became like an exotic, sweet-smelling garden. It smelt so sweet that one wanted to eat it – it was sweeter than jam. All around there was fruit that gleamed like gold.

Suddenly a horrible noise began. It came from the drawer where Hjalmaar had put his school exercise book. When he opened it, Old Shut-Eye saw lots of enormous black letters lying helplessly tangled together among the lines on the page, while a mistake, which had got into a sum, was jumping from place to place, trying to arrive at the right answer. They were all crying out loudly for help.

So Old Shut-Eye took a magic wand, waved it over the book and immediately all the letters stood up straight and tall and the sum solved itself neatly. But alas, when Shut-

golden swords on their shoulders that gleamed in the sunshine. When they lowered their swords showers of sweets and fruit fell from the sky. Princesses came from each palace and gave him sugar hearts and sang him strange and soothing lullabies. It was the most wonderful voyage that Hjalmaar had ever had.

When night fell on Wednesday, rain was pouring down outside. Old Shut-Eye came and opened the window, and Hjalmaar saw a broad lake in the garden, and a noble ship lying close to the house. Shut-Eye invited the little boy to go aboard and, as they sailed along, they saw a number of storks flying past on their way to warmer lands. One of them was so tired that he trailed far behind his friends and finally glided down to land on the deck just at Hjalmaar's feet.

A cabin boy appeared and shut the exhausted stork in a hen-coop with some turkeys and ducks.

'What a strange bird,' said the hen.

'Who are you?' asked a turkey.

Eye had gone away and Hjalmaar awoke in the morning and looked at his book, his homework was as untidy and wretched looking as ever, much to his teacher's distress later that day.

A picture hung over the chest of drawers in Hjalmaar's bedroom. It was a landscape showing a broad river which flowed through a leafy forest, past many castles and far out to sea. When Shut-Eye visited Hjalmaar on Tuesday night, he made his picture come to life. Birds began to sing in the trees and clouds to speed across the blue sky.

Then Shut-Eye lifted little Hjalmaar up and placed him in the picture landscape. He ran to the water's edge and sat down in a little red and white boat which lay there.

Six swans appeared and drew the little boat past the beautiful forest, across an ocean filled with wonderful gleaming fishes to a land of glass and marble palaces. At each palace little princes stood sentry. They had

'A stork, on my way to Africa,' replied the poor bird.

'What did he say?' quacked a duck.

'Don't ask me,' said the turkey. 'He's speaking a very strange language.'

Hjalmaar felt so sorry for the wild bird as it sat dreaming of its family on the warm shores of Africa, that he opened the cage door and set it free. As it flew away, the stork nodded to Hjalmaar as if to thank him.

When he awoke Hjalmaar was astonished to find himself in his own little bed, far from the sea and with not a bird in sight!

On Thursday, Old Shut-Eye brought with him a little mouse, who politely invited Hjalmaar to a wedding which was to take place that very evening under the floorboards in his mother's larder. With a wave of his wand Shut-Eye made Hjalmaar very small and dressed him in a smart new uniform for the occasion.

The little boy travelled to the ceremony in a thimble drawn by the mouse who had invited him. First they came to a long passage

beneath the boards which was only just high enough for them to drive through in the thimble. The whole passage was lit with little glow-worms and was lined with pieces of bacon rind that made the little mouse's mouth water because it smelt so delicious.

Soon he arrived at a great hall where the bride and groom stood in a hollow cheese rind greeting their guests.

The wedding feast consisted entirely of bacon rinds except for the dessert. Then a pea was produced which had been bitten by a relation to show the initials of the couple. Hjalmaar had never seen anything like it – it was a joyous affair and he had a very good time.

Another marriage was to take place on Friday night. The bride and groom were Bertha and Hermann, two big dolls who belonged to Hjalmaar's sister. Shut-Eye himself was to perform the ceremony. Whenever Hjalmaar's sister decided that two of her dolls should get married, Shut-Eye said that he always was asked to perform the ceremony – so he was very experienced.

All the windows of the dolls' cardboard house were lit up for the occasion, and when Hjalmaar and Shut-Eye arrived at the house, the tin soldiers fired a salute. The dolls received many grand presents and a song was sung which had been specially written for them by the coloured pencil.

Soon it was time to set off on their honeymoon. But where should they go? The swallow suggested vineyards and mountains, but the old hen advised that the sand pit in the garden would be much less tiring to get to and just as pleasant.

When Saturday night fell, Old Shut-Eye spread his very finest umbrella over Hjalmaar's head. It looked like a great china bowl with blue trees and pointed bridges with little Chinamen on them, nodding their heads happily. Inviting Hjalmaar to look at this sight, Shut-Eye told him he was too busy to tell him a story that night. Tomorrow was Sunday and a holiday and he must have the world looking bright and pretty on such an important day.

At this, an old portrait of Hjalmaar's great-grandfather came to life and reproached Shut-Eye for confusing the boy with such nonsense. Old Shut-Eye was very offended and he furled his umbrella and went about his important business without another word.

When Old Shut-Eye came on Sunday, he said that tonight he wanted Hjalmaar to meet someone, his brother, whose name was Death.

'What is your brother like?' asked Hjalmaar.

'You will soon see. He is a bit like me,' said Shut-Eye. 'And he only calls on people once.'

'Does he tell stories?' Hjalmaar's eyes were wide with fear.

'He only knows two,' replied Shut-Eye. 'One he tells to good people and it is the most wonderful story ever told.'

'What about the other one?'

'The second he tells to wicked people and it is terrifying.'

But this Death was not terrifying at all. He wore a splendid hussar's uniform with shining silver embroidery, and rode on a noble black horse across the dark blue of the night sky.

'Death is a wonderful creature, Old Shut-Eye!' cried Hjalmaar. 'I shall never be afraid of him again.'

'That's good,' said Shut-Eye, with a kind smile. 'For as long as you continue to be good and work hard at your lessons my brother will welcome you whenever you are ready and tell you even more wonderful stories than I.'

The Shepherdess and the Chimney-Sweep

On a table in a grand drawing room stood a little shepherdess made of china. At her feet lay a tiny lamb and on her head she wore a golden hat with pretty coloured ribbons. She was very lovely. Close by stood another porcelain figure, a little chimney-sweep. His clothes were as black as coal and he carried a small ladder. The two seemed a perfect match – both were young and handsome, and both were very fragile. They were very much in love and wanted to get married.

However, just behind them stood an old porcelain Chinaman,

the shepherdess's grandfather. He was very remarkable and a little frightening – for he could nod his china head.

Now the Chinaman wanted the little shepherdess to marry a figure carved out of the wood of an old oak cupboard who stood nearby. He had goat's legs, little horns and a long beard. The children in the house where the porcelain figures all lived called the strange figure the Billygoat-legs-Major-and-Lieutenant-General-War-Commander-Sergeant. This is a very long name and is very difficult to pronounce, so we won't use it again; we will call him the wooden man.

The shepherdess did not like him at all. But the wooden man was very rich. He had a whole cupboard full of silver plate. . . .

'I won't go into that dark cupboard!' cried the poor little shepherdess. 'I hear he has eleven porcelain wives in there already. I will not be the twelfth.' Her eyes filled with tears.

'But you *will* be the twelfth,' said the obstinate old Chinaman. 'This very night you shall marry him, or else I shall arrange for you to be smashed in pieces.'

With that he nodded his china head, and fell asleep.

On hearing the Chinaman's words, the wooden man smiled gleefully to himself, knowing that in a few hours he would be married to the shepherdess.

The little shepherdess wept bitterly and looked at her beloved chimney-sweep.

'There is nothing for it,' he told her. 'We must escape to the great wide world.'

'But how can we ever get safely down from the table?' asked the shepherdess.

The brave little chimney-sweep comforted her and led the way. He showed her where to place her feet on the carved corners and gilded leaves of the table legs. He brought his ladder too to help her, and soon they stood together, side by side, on the floor.

Hand in hand, they tiptoed stealthily across the room, terrified lest the old Chinaman should wake up and discover they had gone.

The chimney-sweep had an idea for their escape, but he looked at his beloved shepherdess with concern and asked:

'Have you thought how big the world will seem, and that we may never return once we are out there? Do you really want to go on?'

'We have no choice,' replied the shepherdess. And she smiled bravely.

'Then our way lies through the chimney. If we can creep through the stove, I know my way from there. We'll climb so high that no one will ever find us and right at the top there is a hole that leads into the great wide world.'

When she saw the dirty blackness of the stove, the little shepherdess grew pale, but courageously she followed the sweep into the chimney, and the darkness closed in around them.

'But look up there!' cried the chimney-sweep. And, raising her eyes, she saw, far up in the distance, a beautiful star shining in the night sky.

They clambered and crept for many hours. It was frightening, dirty and very dangerous. But the sweep supported and helped his beloved all the way, showing her the best places to put her tiny porcelain feet. So, at last, they reached the top of the chimney. There they rested, for they were desperately tired – as well they might be.

They looked about them – far, far out over the rooftops into the

great unknown world. The poor shepherdess had never imagined anything could be so huge. She was terribly frightened and cried so that the pink of her dress began to run and fall onto the tiles.

'I cannot bear it,' she sobbed. 'The world is too large. If only I had known, I should never have come. If you love me, please take me back to the old table.'

Because he truly loved her, the chimney-sweep agreed, and so with great pain and difficulty they climbed back down the steep and slippery chimney until they stood in the dark stove. All was still and quiet, just as they had left it. They opened the door. . . .

The old Chinaman lay broken in pieces on the floor! His body was quite smashed and his head had rolled into the middle of the room. The wooden man stood where he had always stood, looking on thoughtfully.

'This is terrible!' cried the little shepherdess, wringing her china hands. 'Grandfather has fallen and broken into pieces – and it is all our fault!'

'What can we do?' she wailed. 'Oh if only we had been content with where we were, this need never have happened.'

The chimney-sweep was so upset at seeing how sad his love was that he began to feel guilty at taking her through the stove and up the chimney on to the roof top up above.

Again she turned to him and asked what was to be done.

'Don't worry,' the little chimney-sweep reassured her, 'he can always be repaired.'

The china couple climbed back on to the table.

The Chinaman was duly mended. A great rivet was fastened through his neck: he looked for all the world as good as new, but, in fact, he could no longer nod his head.

After a while, the wooden man said to him:

'You seem to have become very proud since you fell. I wish to know once and for all. Am I to marry your grand-daughter?'

The chimney-sweep and the little shepherdess looked at the old Chinaman fearfully, for they were afraid that he might nod.

The old man's head did not move, not by so much as an inch.

'Have you gone deaf, as well as proud?' asked the wooden man, sounding very cross indeed. 'Answer me. Am I to marry your grand-daughter? I have a place ready for her in my cupboard. Tell me when we can be wed.'

But, as we know, he could not and, as he was unwilling to admit to anyone that he had a rivet in his neck, he remained silent.

So the porcelain couple were married and remained together happily and loved one another faithfully for many a year.

The Lucky Gardener

In the countryside near Copenhagen there stood a tall and stately castle.

All the passers-by admired it for its pointed towers, but, above all, for the perfection of its garden, with its vast lawn, its magnificently ordered rows of bushes and beds ablaze with flowers of many colours.

Inside the castle was equally impressive. Beautiful furniture adorned each room, paintings by the great masters hung on every wall and the family coat of arms appeared in pride of place in the great hall.

The owners of this castle had a highly skilled gardener called

Larsen, who tended the grounds with loving care.

Near the tall entrance gates stood some ancient stark-looking trees. Their ugly appearance distressed Larsen, but mainly it was the raucous cries of the crows which nested in their branches which made him complain to his employers:

'Those old trees should be cut down. It would improve the view and rid us of those noisy birds at the same time.'

His employers, however, did not agree at all.

'Those trees are centuries old,' they cried. 'They belong to the birds. Surely, Larsen, you have enough space in which to practise your skills. The estate is a good size!'

It was indeed big and the owners were really very pleased with Larsen, for he worked hard and skilfully to keep the garden in perfect order. Magnificently-scented flowers grew in abundance and the fruit and vegetables were so delicious they melted in the mouth.

However, one day the lord and lady called their gardener in to the drawing-room and told him, as tactfully as they knew how, that the evening before when they had dined with some neighbours, they had eaten the most delicious apples and pears they had ever tasted.

'It must have been foreign fruit,' said the master. 'It was bought from the best greengrocer in town. Go to his shop tomorrow like a good fellow, Larsen, and find out where it came from. We must get hold of some cuttings and then, of course, your skill will do the rest.'

So Larsen called on the shopkeeper, whom he knew well, for he sold him all the surplus fruit from the castle orchard.

'That fruit came from your own land,' said the man, laughing heartily.

Larsen jumped for joy and hurried back to report the news to

his employers.

'I don't believe it!' cried the lord of the castle. 'Would the greengrocer swear to that? In writing? Go back and ask him.'

Early next day, the faithful servant returned to the town and had no difficulty in obtaining the necessary document.

From that day apples and pears graced every table in the castle. They even sent beautiful basketfuls to friends and relations.

However, just in case the gardener should become too proud of his success, the lord and lady were always careful to remark how favourable the weather had been that year.

A few months passed . . .

The owners of the castle were invited to dine at the palace.

They were given unusually juicy melons served on silver dishes by liveried footmen.

Early next morning Larsen was summoned to the castle drawing-room and told of the events of the previous evening.

'Be a good fellow, Larsen,' said the noble lord, 'and ask the king's gardener for a seed from one of those delicious melons.'

'But . . . my lord . . . I myself supplied the seed,' the poor man stammered nervously.

'Well,' retorted his master, somewhat annoyed. 'I am sure the king's gardener must have used some special treatment to make them so *very* tasty.'

'Your Lordship is mistaken,' replied Larsen. 'When his crop failed, I gave him the melons you ate last night. I will give you written proof of it.'

As soon as they had the document confirming that the melons did indeed originate in their own garden, the lord and lady proudly flourished it before anyone who came to call. Soon their

fruit and vegetables were famous in England and Germany, and seeds and cuttings were sent to countries far away.

Who would have believed such a thing?

'I do hope Larsen will not get too high an opinion of himself and his talents,' murmured the lord of the castle.

Far from becoming lazy and complacent, however, Larsen now worked harder than ever. Every year he produced a new strain and almost always it was a success.

Even so, his employers still insisted that the new apples, pears and melons were never as good as those of the first great year.

True, the strawberries *were* delicious, but so very undistinguished. As for the radishes, one should not even speak of them, they were so horribly small and tasteless.

Several times a week Larsen decorated the great drawing room with flowers. His taste in flower arranging was marvellous, earning complimentary words from the lady of the castle:

'How fortunate you are to have this natural gift, dear Larsen. You achieve such a harmonious effect – and seemingly with no effort at all.'

One morning Larsen brought to the drawing room a single blue flower of a simple but exquisite beauty.

'Oh!' cried his mistress, 'it must be an Indian lotus blossom!' All day long she and her husband admired the flower, carrying it from place to place in the room so that it might always stand in a bright halo of sunlight.

Relations came from all around to see this wonder. Everyone declared they had never seen anything like it, that it must be a rare exotic plant! Finally, the princess herself came to see the extraordinary flower. She left the castle in raptures.

The owners hurriedly sent the flower to the royal palace, for it was truly magnificent, a worthy gift for a princess. This was their chance for glory and they were determined not to miss it.

But they found their drawing room looked quite bare without the blue flower, so they went down into the grounds to pick another to replace it.

They walked the length and breadth of the garden, peering into every flower bed, without success. . . .

Finally, in desperation, they questioned the gardener.

'Ah, the blue flower? It is a very humble plant - but so beautiful. You will find it in the kitchen garden, surrounded by vegetables, for it is an artichoke bloom.'

'For heaven's sake, Larsen!' exclaimed the owners in unison.

'Why didn't you tell us this before? We have presented the blue flower to the king's daughter as if it were an exotic plant. And she is quite a botanist too! Her highness will think we are making fun of her. We will never be received at court again. You have made

fools of us, you wretched man!'

They hurriedly apologised to the princess, blaming their servant for this strange mistake. They assured her, moreover, that the man had been severely reprimanded.

On reading the letter, the princess exclaimed:

'How unfair! The gardener is obviously a poet at heart. He has revealed to us the beauty of a simple plant. From now until they cease to bloom, I shall have an artichoke flower brought to me every day for the drawing room.'

This was duly done . . . and the castle owners rushed to restore the blue flower to its pride of place in their own drawing room.

117

Larsen himself received many compliments.

'Our gardener enjoys his praise,' his master was heard to mutter, 'just like a spoilt child.'

Autumn came. The leaves fell. . . wind, rain and fog surrounded the castle.

One evening a great storm blew up. The tall trees which housed the crows' nests were battered by a ferocious wind. All through the night the birds were heard calling shrilly in terror as they were blown headlong against the castle windows. What a night that was!

'Well, Larsen,' said the owners the next morning, 'you have what you wanted. Now there is plenty of room for your grand ideas. It's a pity though. We always loved those old trees.'

The gardener did not answer, but walked slowly towards where the poor trees lay broken and twisted on the ground.

For many days he was to be seen striding through the forests and fields of the district. Clearly an idea was buzzing in his head.

When the trees had been cleared away, the banks hoed and raked, Larsen sketched his plan on paper. No one had ever thought of such an idea before. He planted wild juniper, bright green holly and tall ferns that looked like palm trees. Here and

there he scattered clumps of wild flowers and woodland plants. The effect was as charming as it was artistic.

It was nearly Christmas and, as was the custom in Denmark, a tall pole was erected to fly the Danish flag. Larsen chose to put his flagpole where the old trees had been. Around its top he built a ledge on which he laid a sheaf of corn so that the birds could share in the feasting . . .

The owners were a little jealous of Larsen when everyone began to talk about how successful his scheme was. Although they pretended to be grateful, they weren't at all. Although they could have dismissed him they never did for, as they said to themselves, they were *far* too kind-hearted to do that!

119

The Wild Swans

Far, far away in the land where the swallows fly to in winter, lived a rich widower king with his eleven sons and his little daughter, Eliza.

One day, the king told his children that he was going to marry again. Unfortunately, the new queen was a very cruel, jealous woman, and she hated the children right from the beginning.

She began to tell the king evil lies about his sons, so that finally he believed her and banished them all from the kingdom. As they left, their stepmother cursed them, saying:

'Fly away like great dumb birds. You must earn your own living from now on.'

Immediately, the princes were transformed into eleven magnificent wild swans which flew gracefully out of the palace windows and disappeared over the sea.

As for little Eliza, she too couldn't do anything right and was sent away to the country to be brought up by a humble peasant family.

Several years passed and when she was fifteen, the young princess returned to the palace, for the king wished to see her. She was now very beautiful, and when the wicked queen saw this, she became very jealous and her heart filled with hatred.

Early the next morning, the queen entered Eliza's bathroom. In it stood a white marble bath, surrounded by soft cushions and splendid tapestries. Into this beautiful scene, the queen brought three hideous toads. She kissed them and placed them one by one in the clear water, saying to the first:

'Sit on the child's head so that she may become as stupid as
you,' and to the second, 'Sit on her forehead that she may become
as ugly as you.' To the third she whispered, 'Rest on her heart so
that she may be filled with evil thoughts and her life be nothing
but misery and bitterness.'

When Eliza came to take her bath, the toads did as they had
been told, but the beautiful princess did not seem to notice them
and as she emerged, three lovely red roses were observed floating
on the water. The evil toads had no power over this good and
innocent child and had been turned into objects of beauty by her
sweetness and virtue.

The queen saw what had happened and flew into a fury. She
took Eliza and smeared her face with stinging walnut oil so that
her skin became stained and ugly. Her hair she tangled into knots,

so that by the end poor Eliza was quite unrecognizable. The king, when he saw her, thought she was just an ugly peasant child, and threw her from the court to face the world alone.

Poor Eliza wandered miserably throughout the land, not knowing which way to turn. When she saw her reflection in the surface of a great lake, she was horrified. But when she bathed her face in a little water her true perfection was again revealed and a more beautiful princess could not have been found in the whole world.

Later she came upon an old woman who fed her with delicious berries and told her how she had seen eleven swans, with golden

crowns on their heads, swimming in the lake the day before. Eliza had no doubt that these were her poor brothers and she wept bitterly to think that she had missed them.

But just as the sun was setting, there was a great sound like rushing wind and she saw the swans alighting near her. Darkness fell and suddenly their feathers fell from them and there stood eleven handsome princes. Eliza hurried to embrace them, for she immediately recognized her brothers, although they were now fine young men.

The eldest prince soon began to explain to little Eliza the cruel fate which their stepmother had imposed on them:

'During the day we are free to fly as wild swans wherever we please, so long as we never enter our dear homeland. By nightfall, however, we must be on dry land, for then we resume our human forms until the first rays of the sun make us feathered prisoners once more.'

'How do you come to be here now? Are you not in mortal danger, coming into the land from which you have been banished?' asked Eliza anxiously.

'No, for once a year we are permitted to visit our dear old home. For eleven days only we may stay here and this is the eleventh day. Tomorrow we must depart. We cannot bear the thought of losing you again. Have you the courage to fly with us?'

Eliza did not hesitate, so the next morning, carrying their beloved sister in a fine white sheet, the swans flew high up towards the clouds. For a while the sun shone directly into her face, blinding her, until her youngest brother, noticing her distress, flew above her head so that his broad wing shaded her

pretty golden head and beautiful face from the burning rays.

They flew for what seemed a very long time. Eliza began to worry in case her extra weight was slowing the swans down and preventing them from reaching their destination before the sun set and they became men again.

However, as twilight approached the swans swiftly swooped down and gently placed their precious burden in front of a great

cave overgrown with beautiful plants. Here they left her to rest, until they could safely bring her to their new home.

As she lay waiting for sleep to come, Eliza prayed that she might dream of a way to release her dear brothers from the spell that bound them.

As soon as she was asleep, it seemed to Eliza that a beautiful fairy stood before her, radiant and tall. When she spoke Eliza was reminded of the kind woman who had given her berries on the day of her flight from the palace.

'If you have courage and determination, your brothers can be freed,' said the fairy. 'You must pick the stinging nettles that grow just outside this cave, though they will burn your hands into blisters. Then you must break them up with your feet, spin them into flaxen thread and weave eleven shirts. Throw these over the swans and the cruel spell will be broken. But remember also,' warned the fairy, 'that until the shirts are finished you must not speak one word, or your brothers will surely die.'

As soon as she awoke, Eliza began to do as the fairy had instructed. Her hands and feet were soon covered with agonizing blisters, but when her brothers returned and enquired anxiously what she was doing, she was dumb. The youngest wept sadly, and where his tears fell on her hands, the burning blisters vanished.

The next day, a hunting horn sounded and the king of the country appeared riding with his hounds and spotted the beautiful girl among the nettles. The king was enchanted by Eliza's beauty and her mysterious silent work among the cruel weeds, and he carried her off with him to his palace, wishing to make her his bride.

Everyone at the court was dazzled by Eliza's beauty and took her to their hearts. Everyone, that is, except a mean old courtier who muttered that the dumb girl was obviously a witch who had cast a spell over the king.

As the days went by, Eliza's heart warmed to the handsome young king. She truly loved him, but still she could not tell him the secret of her grief – the fear that she would never see her brothers again, or complete the shirts that were to release them from the wicked old queen's spell. For a single word would cost the princes their lives.

The king had ordered that all the nettles and flax be brought from Eliza's cave to the palace and stored in a special chamber, as a memorial of the scene in which he first found his love. Every night Eliza crept away to this room and wove one more shirt. One night, however, she found that there was no more flax, and she had still three shirts left to weave. How was she to obtain nettles in the well-ordered gardens of the palace? Then she remembered a haunted churchyard the king had told her about. It was a place no one dared venture and only nettles and other savage weeds grew there.

Silently, she stole into the churchyard and gathered the cruel stinging nettles. Unfortunately, the mean courtier had heard her footsteps and he led the king to the churchyard where he could see the young girl happily walking through the haunted place. Then the poor king was deceived, and truly believed that Eliza must be a witch.

She was brought to trial and condemned to be burnt at the stake. The king was heartbroken and Eliza could speak no word in her defence, but only continue to weave the nettle flax as fast as she could.

Even as the hour of execution approached, Eliza was weaving, anxiously trying to finish the last shirt. Suddenly, eleven great swans appeared and surrounded the scaffold. Just as the executioner seized her hand, Eliza threw the shirts over the eleven swans and immediately there stood her tall and handsome brothers. One, however, still had a swan's wing instead of an arm, for, in her haste, she had not finished one of the shirts.

'Now at last I can speak,' she cried. 'I am innocent!' Quickly she told the king and court the whole story.

The king was overjoyed and embraced the princess and her brothers. Then the people bore the brave and beautiful girl high in triumph, the church bells rang and the birds came in great flocks to join the procession. Eliza and the king were soon married and the celebrations continued throughout eleven days and nights.

The Emperor's New Clothes

Once upon a time there lived an emperor. He loved new clothes so passionately that he spent all his money on them. He never went to the theatre, or gave grand banquets, but he had a different coat for every hour of the day. People might normally say of a ruler: 'He is in council,' but in the emperor's court it would be said: 'He is in the wardrobe.'

Two clever villains heard about the emperor's passion and one day they came to the great palace and declared that they could weave clothes from a material finer and more exquisite than anything that had ever been seen in the history of tailoring. Not only were the colours and patterns of this material incredibly beautiful, they said, but it also possessed an extraordinary, magical quality: it became invisible to anyone who was unfit for the office he held, or who was totally stupid.

When the emperor heard of this, he rubbed his hands with glee.

'I must have a suit made with this material,' he thought to himself. 'It is only right that an emperor should have a suit of such fine material and besides, it will be useful to know who is unfit for office or very stupid. Send for the weavers at once!' he said out loud.

The villains told the emperor that the cost of the material was very high, and named such an extortionate price that several chamberlains fainted. But the emperor agreed at once and ordered sacks of silver and gold to be brought and two looms set up at once. The villains immediately began pretending to work, promising to produce their finest ever work for the emperor. And every day for several weeks a further supply of gold and silver was brought to them by the emperor's servants, which they duly pocketed, laughing merrily to themselves in secret.

After a while, the emperor's curiosity was so great that he decided he must have a report on the weaver's progress. For some mysterious reason, he was unwilling to examine the magical material himself, so he sent his wisest and most trusted old minister instead.

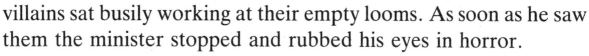

The minister went to the great chamber where the two villains sat busily working at their empty looms. As soon as he saw them the minister stopped and rubbed his eyes in horror.

'Good heavens!' he thought to himself, 'what can this mean? I can't see anything there at all!' But he said nothing out loud.

The villains cordially invited the old man to examine the material closely and, pointing to their empty looms, they asked him if he did not admire the wonderful colours and fine patterns they had woven. The minister stared and stared, but still he could see nothing – which was not at all surprising, since there *was* nothing there to be seen.

'After all these years,' he thought to himself sadly, 'am I now to admit before the whole world that I am stupid and unfit to be the emperor's minister? Impossible!'

So when the mischievous villains eagerly asked him what he thought, he replied at once:

'Oh, it is charming – quite enchanting!' He peered with great concentration through his spectacles and added: 'Such an intricate design – well, I've never seen anything like it. I am sure the emperor will be delighted.'

'So glad you like it,' said both the weavers, and they proceeded to describe the patterns and colours of their imaginary work so vividly that the minister almost – but not quite – began to see them himself.

Soon the whole country was talking about the emperor's marvellous new clothes. Finally, the emperor himself went to visit the weavers at their work, taking with him a whole crowd of excited courtiers and statesmen.

'Isn't it the loveliest garment you have ever seen?' asked the old minister who had visited the chamber before. Everyone looked at the emperor. . . .

'What's this?' thought the royal personage desperately. 'Why, I can see nothing at all. This is disastrous! I am the emperor – and yet, I must be . . . unthinkable! – Oh! it is very pretty indeed,' he said aloud. Then with more confidence: 'It has our exalted favour.' And he nodded vigorously, gazing at thin air in an effort to look as if indeed he saw something there of wondrous and rare beauty.

All at once everyone who had been silent and mystified, broke out in a chorus of exclamations: 'How gorgeous!' 'Magnificent! Remarkable! Splendid!' they cried. But none of them saw anything, for, as we know, there *was* nothing to see.

There was general rejoicing and the emperor gave the villains the title of 'Imperial Court Weavers'. He declared that he would wear his splendid new clothes for the first time at the great procession that was to take place the following morning.

The villains promised to 'work' all through the night to complete the clothes and, shortly before dawn, they were observed taking the non-existent material down from the looms. They cut the thin air with great scissors and sewed it using needles without any thread. At last they announced that all was ready . . .

The emperor came for a fitting. He took off his old clothes. Soon he was standing in only his underwear. The first cheat helped the emperor into a 'shirt'.

'Has your Majesty ever worn a shirt so light and of such splendid colour?' he asked.

'Never,' replied the emperor, and turning to the courtiers he asked them the same question.

'It is wonderful,' said one courtier.

'The colour is so subtle,' said another.

The second cheat helped the emperor into his breeches.

'Has your majesty ever worn such breeches?' he asked.

'Never,' replied the emperor.

'And the colour is a perfect complement to the shirt.'

'Perfect,' said the emperor.

'Absolutely perfect,' murmured the courtier.

'Wait until your Majesty tries on the waistcoat and coat,' said the first cheat, pretending to hold the waistcoat out, but really holding thin air.

The emperor shrugged his shoulders as if he was pulling on a waistcoat and coat. 'There,' he said, standing in his underwear, 'How do I look?'

'Splendid,' said the first cheat.

'Regal,' said the second.

'How does it feel?' asked the first.

'Is it comfortable?' asked the second.

'It's as light as a spider's web: you would think you had nothing on; but that is just the beauty of it,' said the first.

'Yes, indeed,' said all the courtiers attending; but they could not see anything there at all.

The emperor stood before his great mirror, appearing to look with pleasure on his new clothes.

The chamberlains whose job it was to carry the emperor's train in the grand procession stooped down just as if they were picking up the mantle. They did not dare let it be noticed that they saw nothing.

As the emperor walked ceremonially through the streets of the city, everyone exclaimed loudly, 'How splendid the emperor's new clothes are! How well they fit him!' No one wanted to be thought stupid or unfit for his job. None of the emperor's previous clothes had had such universal success.

'I've never seen the emperor look so handsome,' remarked one old lady to another, 'and I've seen him every day for as long as I can remember.'

'The emperor looks so handsome,' said her companion who was very deaf.

'I have just said that,' said the first old lady.

'Yes, very handsome,' said the second.

Then the emperor passed a small child standing with his father in the shadow of a poor building. The child took one look at the

emperor and exclaimed to the embarrassment of his father:

'But – he has got nothing on at all!'

The emperor heard the cry and stopped abrupty – for it seemed to him suddenly that perhaps the child was right. . . .

But then he remembered his superior importance and held his head high, thinking to himself, 'The procession must go on.'

And so the chamberlains continued to hold on to thin air tighter than ever and the emperor and his admiring train proceeded in dignified procession through the town.

The Little Match Girl

One freezing cold New Year's Eve, as the snow swirled
mercilessly through the dark streets of a big city, a poor little
match girl, bareheaded and barefoot, trudged wearily home-
wards.

Shivering with cold and hunger, she crept among the richly
dressed folk who were so occupied with their own concerns that
they failed to notice the tiny huddled figure. The snow flakes
settled in her long hair as she struggled on towards the cold and
cheerless hovel where her father would surely beat her. He would
be angry, for she had not sold a single bundle of matches all day.
People had been too busy planning the gorgeous feasts they would
be enjoying that night to think of helping the poor little match girl

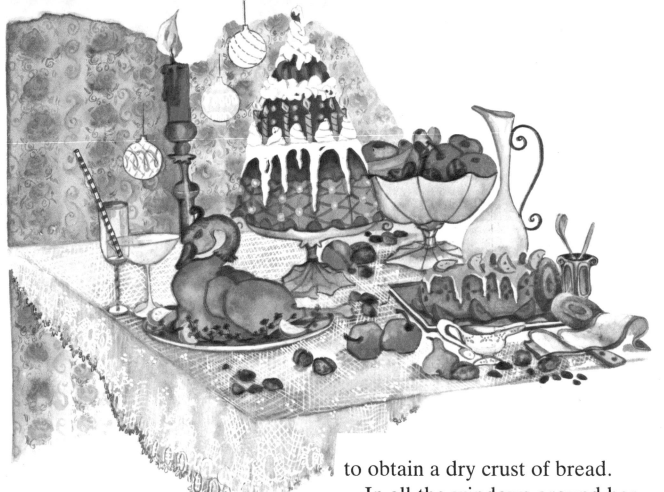

to obtain a dry crust of bread.

In all the windows around her now lights were shining brightly and there was a delicious smell of roasting goose in the cold night air. This made the little girl's hunger all the harder to bear, so that she sank down, exhausted and despairing, in the inadequate shelter of the angle between two adjoining houses.

Her little hands were almost entirely numb with cold. Perhaps if she could find the strength to light one of the matches she carried it would bring some warmth back into her frozen fingers. With difficulty she drew one out and struck it against the cold stone wall behind her. By its flickering light – which seemed all at once to the little match girl wonderfully bright – she saw before her a polished iron stove, glowing with inviting heat. But, as she stretched out her hands towards the vision, the little flame went out and she was left with only a burnt up match.

She struck a second match and, as it flared, the wall beside her

146

appeared to become transparent and she could see right into the room inside. On the table a snowy white cloth was laden with shining silver piled high with cakes and fruit and, in the centre, an enormous roast goose. To her astonishment, the little match girl saw the goose suddenly spring off its dish and move towards her. At that moment the match went out and only the thick damp wall was before her.

She lit another match – and suddenly she was sitting under a beautiful Christmas tree. It was tall and dazzling with decorations and candles and around it were piled all the playthings she had

ever seen through the windows of the town toyshops. But no sooner had she exclaimed with joy than a gust of icy wind blew out the third match.

As it did so, it seemed to the little match girl that, instead of fading like the others visions, the Christmas tree lights rose higher and higher into the air until they twinkled as stars in the sky; one of them fell down, drawing after it a long tail of fire.

'That means someone is dying,' thought the little match girl. For her grandmother, the only person who had ever loved her and who was now dead herself, had told her that whenever a star fell down, a soul rose up to God.

She struck another match against the wall. In the brightness that followed she clearly saw her beloved grandmother standing, smiling, before her.

'Grandmother!' cried the little match girl delightedly, and hurriedly she struck the whole bundle of matches together, so that she might keep her grandmother with her for as long as possible. The matches burned with such a glow that the light was as bright as the midday sun. In the middle of it stood the grandmother, tall and radiant. She smiled again and, taking the little match girl in her arms, flew far above the earth to a place of eternal peace.

Ib and Christine

In a farmhouse, in the middle of a forest in northern Jutland, lived the Jeppe-Jans family. They kept a pig and two oxen and, in the summer, cultivated the sandy soil of the fields round about. In the winter Mr. Jeppe-Jans carved wooden shoes which were strong and light and graceful.

At the time this story begins the only child of the family, a little boy called Ib, was seven years old. He had one great friend in all the world, the boatman's pretty little daughter, Christine. The two were always together; they shared their bread and berries when they were very hungry, and the first pair of wooden shoes that Ib ever made he gave to little Christine.

One day, when Christine's father had to deliver some firewood to a neighbouring village, he invited Ib to accompany him and his daughter in the boat. They travelled swiftly downstream, past pools of glowing water lilies to the great weir, where the water rushed through the flood gates with a great roaring noise.

After Christine's father had unloaded the firewood, he bought a sucking pig which he placed in a basket in the bottom of the boat while he went off to see some friends. He told the children to sit quietly until he returned, but soon they became bored and Ib opened the basket and picked up the sucking pig to admire its size and dream of the delicious meal that it was going to make. But – much to his horror – it slipped through his hands and was carried away downstream.

The two children immediately jumped out of the boat and tried to follow the pig's progress down the river. But they were soon deep in an unfamiliar wood and could no longer see either the boat or the bank. Christine tripped and fell to the ground. She was tired and frightened and began to cry. But Ib picked her up and said stoutly:

'Don't worry. Follow me. I know the way.'

But they wandered on and on, further and further from the river. The fierce cry of an eagle sent them scurrying for cover; a

horrid great owl flew past with a terrifying beating of wings; worst
of all was the thought of the terrible trouble they would get into
for losing the precious sucking pig. By the time it grew dark, they
were completely lost and thoroughly miserable. They threw
themselves down together on a heap of dry leaves and sobbed
themselves to sleep.

When they awoke they were startled to find a tall old woman
standing over them. Her face was burnt dark brown, her hair was
deep black and shining. On her back was a bundle and in her hand
a gnarled staff. She was a gipsy.

At first the children were frightened, but the old woman had
friendly eyes and when she offered them some nuts out of her
pocket their hunger overcame their fear. The old woman told
them, however, that these were wishing nuts, far too precious for
eating. The children's eyes opened wide with wonder and
excitement.

'Is there a carriage with a pair of horses in this nut?' asked Ib.

'Yes – a great carriage made of solid gold,' replied the gipsy.

'Then give me the nut,' said little Christine, her eyes shining.

'This nut,' whispered Ib, concentrating hard, 'contains a beautiful silk scarf, I'm sure of it.'

'Ten such scarves,' answered the old woman, 'together with beautiful dresses and shoes and a hat with silken ribbons.'

'Then I should have that one too,' said Christine.

Ib gave her the second nut. The third was small and black.

'You can keep that one,' said the little girl.

'What is in it?' asked Ib.

'The best gift of all for you,' replied the old woman mysteriously.

Ib held on to the nut very tightly and eventually the old woman led them on to a path that Ib recognized as leading towards his home. Then she vanished as suddenly as she had appeared.

As soon as he was alone Ib cracked open the little black nut the gipsy had given him. Inside was only blackness and a dust that looked like earth. It was just a hollow, worm-eaten old nut after all. He was sorry that Christine would have no fine clothes or a grand carriage, but they were quite happy as they were.

Several years passed. Ib grew into a fine young man and, when his father died, the care of the farm and the wooden shoe-making craft became his responsibility. Meanwhile, Christine was sent to be a servant in a rich merchant's household.

The young people were now separated, but news reached Ib of Christine's good fortune, as her employers took her more and more to their hearts, treating her almost as one of the family, and giving her fine new gowns. Ib was delighted by her success.

One day in the spring, the door of Ib's humble home sprang open and there stood Christine. But she looked so different! She was as elegant and beautiful as a real lady. Ib was speechless, standing there in his muddy working clothes. But Christine seemed as friendly and loving as ever. By the end of an hour, Ib had determined that before she left again he would ask Christine to marry him. It seemed the most natural thing in the world.

'Let us wait for a while, dear Ib,' was her answer. 'I think that I

love you – but I must be sure.' And with that they parted once more.

Another year passed by, during which the two wrote to each other, signing their letters 'faithful unto death'.

Then one day Christine's father came to visit Ib, bearing a message from his daughter. He began talking with difficulty, and was clearly embarrassed and uncomfortable. It seemed that the eldest son of the family in which Christine was living had come home on a visit from Copenhagen and had fallen in love with Christine. He was a fine and clever young man and it would be an ideal match. But Christine had not forgotten her promise to Ib and would not consent unless he released her.

Ib had gone as white as a sheet, but he nodded his head slowly and said:

'Christine must not pass up this chance of fortune and happiness.'

With great pain and difficulty he wrote this letter to his beloved Christine:

Your father has told me the news. This is a great chance for you. Do not think of me. I have so little to offer you myself; you must think of your own future. Do not feel bound to me. I release you from any promise. May every happiness be yours.

Ever your devoted friend,
Ib

So Christine married the young man and went to live in Copenhagen. Ib continued to work on the farm, but he became more and more silent and solitary. A little while later news reached him that the rich merchant had died, leaving Christine's young husband all his money. Then he remembered what the old

gipsy's wishing nuts had promised – now Christine would have all that, and more.

The following spring, as Ib was working in his field, his plough hit a piece of metal which gleamed brightly. It was a great gold armband – one of many valuable treasures in a 'Hun's Grave' which he had stumbled upon.

'The best gift of all!' he thought to himself. 'And I discovered it in the darkness of the earth. The gipsy was right for me, too.'

Ib sailed to Copenhagen to exchange his treasure for gold coins – many bags of them. On the day he was to return home, he became lost in the back streets of the city. He found himself in a very poor area, surrounded by wretched houses and beggars.

A child blundered into him, weak from lack of food. Setting her on her feet, he saw with a shock by the light of a street lamp, the very image of his childhood's sweetheart, little Christine.

He followed the little girl into a wretched house and up a

narrow rickety staircase to a freezing dark chamber under the roof. There, on a poor bed of straw, lay the child's mother, sick with a terrible fever. As he raised her head to give her a drink of water, he saw – it *was* Christine!

Her husband's new-found wealth had made him proud and cruel. He had abandoned Christine and her young child in order to travel the world. Having squandered all his money, deserted by all his friends, he got into debt and finally threw himself into the canal and drowned. Christine had been left in dire poverty.

Seeing that his old love was dying, Ib tearfully promised to care for her little daughter and see that she grew up in comfort and safety. Whether Christine ever realized who he was, Ib never knew. But he carried home with him the little girl who was to make the rest of his life happier and richer by far than all the gold he had found could ever have done. Truly, *this* was 'the best gift of all', and his beloved Christine had given it to him.

The Snow Queen

One day long ago a particularly wicked goblin made a mirror which shrank everything good and beautiful it reflected to almost nothing. Whatever was worthless or ugly, however, became more obvious and more hideous in this distorting glass. All the other goblins thought this a great joke and they flew up to heaven carrying the mirror, so that they could sneer and scoff at the angels themselves. But the mirror fell to the ground, where it shattered into a hundred million million fragments.

Some of these tiny specks of glass flew about in the world causing great unhappiness. For whenever they flew into anyone's eye, they stuck there and, from then on, that person could see only the bad in everything and everyone. Worse still, if a fragment became lodged in someone's heart, then at once it turned into a block of ice.

163

Now we shall hear the story of one such unfortunate child . . .

In a great city stood two tall houses opposite each other. The street was so narrow at this point that the top windows were only a foot apart. In each window was a box filled in summer with beautiful fragrant roses. One day the owners of the houses decided to join the two boxes together across a water pipe, forming a splendid triumphal arch of flowers and leaves.

In the left-hand house lived a little girl called Gerda, while in the house opposite lived Kay, a little boy of the same age. They loved each other like brother and sister. For hours at a time they talked and played together across the flower arch, in summer tending the roses with loving care.

In winter, however, this game came to an end. Sometimes the windows were quite frozen over. Then each of the children would warm a coin on the stove and place it against the glass, making a round peep hole through which they could smile at each other.

Sometimes Kay would visit Gerda in her house, where she lived with her old grandmother. One day, as the snow was falling heavily outside, the old woman was talking to the children:

'Those are the white bees swarming,' she said. 'The queen is there among them, she is the largest bee of all. She will never stay on the ground, but flies up again to the black cloud above. Sometimes she flies through the streets looking in through the windows. Her breath freezes into those strange shapes you may

sometimes have seen which look like pretty flowers on the panes.'

Back again in his own house, Kay looked through the peep hole in the window. Suddenly one snow flake appeared to grow larger and larger. At last he saw it was a beautiful woman dressed in the finest white gauze made of millions of glittering flakes. Her eyes flashed like two clear stars. The Snow Queen! She nodded and beckoned to Kay to follow her. But he was frightened and ran away from the window.

Soon the spring came and the children could sit again at their

rose-filled windows, tending, watering and admiring their flowers.

One day, as they sat together looking at a picture book, Kay felt something strike him in the chest and prick his eye. Poor Kay! A fragment from the wicked goblin's mirror had lodged in his heart and a speck was embedded in his eye.

'Why did you hit me and blow dust into my eye, you silly girl?' he cried to Gerda crossly. 'Anyway, this is a stupid book and these roses have an awful smell. I'm going to play with the other boys. I can't waste my time with babies like you.'

During the next few weeks the change in Kay became more and more marked. For his heart was now like a block of ice and his eyes could see only the bad in everything and everyone.

Winter came again and one day, as Kay was tobogganing in the great square of the city, a large white sled drew up beside him and

166

the driver motioned Kay to hitch a ride by tying his tiny sled to the great one. Kay was delighted and did so at once. The great white sled raced faster and faster. The snow began to fall thicker and faster, until the now-terrified little boy could see no more than an inch in front of him.

All at once the great sled stopped and the driver approached him. It was a *lady*, tall, slender and brilliantly beautiful: the Snow Queen!

'You are cold,' she said. 'Come, share my furs.'

But as she brought him into her own sled, he felt as if he sank

into a great snow drift. The Snow Queen kissed him and he felt as if his soul was turned to ice. Then he forgot little Gerda, the dear window boxes of his home and his whole past life, and the great white sled carried him away into the night.

Meanwhile, Gerda wept long and bitterly, for everyone said that Kay must have drowned in the great river. One morning she went down to its banks to search for a trace of her little friend. She crept into a small boat that lay there, but it was not securely moored and she was carried far away downstream.

She was rescued by an old woman, who welcomed her kindly into a magnificent garden. She gave Gerda cherries and combed

170

her hair with a magic comb which made her forget all her cares and worries. One day a picture of a lovely rose brought back the memory of little Kay. She was filled with remorse at the time she had wasted. Thanking the old woman for her kindness, Gerda set out through the snow to look for Kay.

One day, as she rested, trembling with cold and hunger, Gerda saw a great crow sitting nearby, looking at her.

'Krah! Krah! What are you doing out alone in the snow?' asked the friendly bird.

It did not pronounce very well, but Gerda understood the word

'alone' and all that it meant. She told the crow the whole story of her life and asked if he had seen Kay.

'Possibly. My sweetheart is the royal crow and she has told me recently of a young man as clever and brave as the one you describe who arrived at the palace some time ago and married the young princess.'

'Oh, it's him, I'm sure it's Kay!' cried Gerda excitedly. 'Please, Mr. Crow, won't you take me to the palace with you so that I may make quite certain?'

The kind crow agreed and that night, when it was dark, he led Gerda to the back door which stood ajar. Gerda's heart beat fast with hope and fear! The royal crow met them and led Gerda to the great bedchamber where the prince lay sleeping. As she gently pulled aside the curtain round the prince's bed, he awoke, turned his head, and – alas, it was not little Kay!

Poor disappointed Gerda! She wept and wept. But the prince listened sympathetically to her story and, when he had rewarded the crows for their kindness, he clothed Gerda in fur boots, gave her a warm muff and provided a gold carriage to take her once more on her quest for little Kay.

A little further on, however, Gerda was seized by a band of robbers who had seen the gleaming gold of the carriage. Just as a fearsome old woman was about to kill poor Gerda, a dark-haired little girl bit her sharply in the arm so that she dropped the cruel knife with a cry of pain:

'I want her,' said the girl. 'She shall give me her muff and I will play with her and not kill her as long as she is good.'

So Gerda was taken to the robbers' castle. Inside a great cauldron bubbled ominously and spiders' webs and caged pigeons hung from the beams overhead. These were the robber girl's pets and she introduced them all to little Gerda.

'This is my favourite, old Ba,' she said, indicating a great
reindeer tethered in the corner. 'Every night I tickle him with this
knife – he's very frightened of that.' The girl laughed and turned
back to the now terrified Gerda, saying, 'Now, tell me your story.'

So Gerda told all about the garden, the palace and the crow,
and her search for little Kay, so that even the robber girl's hard
little heart melted with sympathy. At one point, the caged pigeons
called out, 'Coo! coo! we have seen little Kay. A white wolf
carried his sled and he rode in the Snow Queen's carriage. She
was taking him to her great ice castle in Lapland.'

At this the old reindeer sighed deeply. 'That is a fine country.
There's ice and snow all the year round and you can run free in
the great glittering plains. I know, for I was born and bred there.'

Suddenly the robber girl sprang up. 'Well, that settles it. Since
old Ba knows the way, he must take you to Lapland, Gerda, and

then, although I do so enjoy tickling him with my knife, he may as well go free.'

The reindeer sprang high into the air with joy and Gerda kissed the little robber girl in gratitude. Then quickly they left.

The reindeer ran hard day and night, far over marshes and steppes till it came to a little hut, where a tiny Lapland woman stood stirring a cooking pot.

'O wise old woman of Lapland,' said the reindeer. 'I know you can tie all the winds of the world together with a bit of twine, won't you give this little girl a potion so that she may have strength to overcome the Snow Queen and set her friend Kay free?'

'She needs no help from me,' said the old woman. 'She possesses all the power she needs inside herself. For her love and sweetness alone will melt the ice from Kay's heart and keep them both from the Snow Queen's icy clutches. Her castle is nearby. Hurry, for there is no time to lose.'

It grew darker and much, much colder – and in her haste Gerda had forgotten her warm boots so that soon her feet were quite numb with cold. Soon they were approaching the vast and empty halls of the Snow Queen's palace, so Gerda dismounted and said goodbye to the reindeer who had served her so well.

Inside, in a great chamber of glittering ice Gerda found little Kay, standing motionless and quite blue with cold. She flew into his arms and held him tight, but he was quite stiff. Then she wept hot tears and, as they fell upon his chest, they melted the lump of ice that lay in his heart. Kay too began to shed tears of joy at seeing Gerda and so the splinter of glass was washed from his eye.

The warmth of the children's joy was so great that the great blocks of ice about them began to melt, and soon the whole of the Snow Queen's palace had disappeared. Gerda had won at last!

Jack the Dunce

Once upon a time in a far distant country there lived an old baron. He had two sons who thought themselves too clever by half.

When the king's daughter publicly announced that she would choose for her husband the man who could speak the most fluently, these two geniuses immediately began to prepare for the test. One learnt the whole Latin dictionary and three years' issues of the local daily paper by heart. The other became so learned in the laws of the land that he was sure he could speak wisely on any affair of state. Each was equally certain that he would win the princess.

The day came for the wooing and the baron gave each of his clever sons a handsome horse. To the Latin scholar he gave a jet black steed, to the lawyer a white. Then they rubbed the corners of their mouths with fish oil so that they might talk the more smoothly and fluently.

All the servants had gathered in the courtyard to watch the

177

grand pair set off. By chance the baron's third son appeared on the scene. No one had thought of him entering the contest for the princess, for he was not nearly so clever as his two brothers, and indeed was generally known as Jack the Dunce. But this youngest son had other ideas.

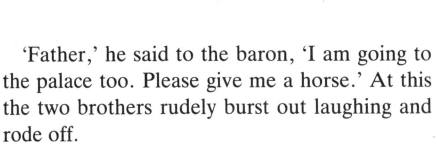

'Father,' he said to the baron, 'I am going to the palace too. Please give me a horse.' At this the two brothers rudely burst out laughing and rode off.

'Nonsense,' replied the baron crossly. 'You shall have no horse from me. You can hardly string two words together. Your brothers are fine, educated fellows, but you – you had far better stay at home and mind the pigs.'

'Well,' said Jack the Dunce, quite unabashed,

'if I can't have a horse, Ill ride there on my billy goat. He will serve just as well.'

Quickly he mounted the goat and galloped off down the street whooping and cheering with excitement and high spirits.

When he caught up with his brothers, he found them strangely silent and thoughtful. They were carefully planning the fine speeches they would make to the princess.

Meanwhile, Jack the Dunce was doing some very strange things. He kept stopping to pick up objects he found lying by the wayside: a dead crow, an old wooden shoe. He even filled his pockets with clay out of the ditch. His brothers laughed scornfully and mocked him. What an idiot he was, they thought to themselves smugly. And they galloped on ahead, arriving at the palace a whole hour earlier than Jack.

At the gate each suitor was given a number and made to wait in line until he was called by a liveried footman. This made all the suitors very nervous.

At last it was the turn of the eldest brother, that famous Latin scholar. He was shown into a huge chamber. Its walls were lined with mirrors, so that he could see himself from every angle. At the window stood several people waiting to take down every word he uttered to

report throughout the kingdom. Somehow or other, he found he could not remember a single syllable of English, let alone Latin. Moreover, the stove had been stoked so that it gave off a colossal heat. Finally, in desperation:

'It is dreadfully hot in here!' he exclaimed.

'Yes,' replied the princess, 'my father is going to roast chickens.'

When he opened his mouth to respond wittily to this odd remark, only a strangled bleat came out, and the princess stamped her foot impatiently, crying, 'He's no use! Take him away!'

Now the second brother came in, full of confidence in his legal learning. But: 'Oh dear! What a heat!' he exclaimed.

'Yes, we're roasting chickens today,' said the princess.

'What? – what did you – er – sorry?' stammered the second brother. And the writers scribbled gleefully 'wh – what – er – sorry' in there notebooks.

'Hopeless. Take him away!' cried the princess.

Now came the turn of Jack the Dunce still on his goat.

'Well, it's most incredibly hot in here,' he cried cheerfully.

'Yes, because I'm roasting chickens,' replied the princess.

'That's a bit of luck!' exclaimed Jack, 'for I have here a crow that I should like to roast at the same time with your permission.'

'By all means,' said the princess, 'but I have no cooking pot.'

'No matter. Here's something that will do.' And he pulled out the wooden shoe. 'Now a little sauce,' bringing some of the clay from his pockets, 'and we have a dish fit for royalty!'

'I like it,' said the princess, laughing merrily. 'You are ingenious and have something to say for yourself. But did you know that everything you say is being written down?'

'Oh, those are the gentlemen over there, are they?' said Jack, looking mischievous. 'Well, I have an extra something left for them. Let them print *this* in their newspaper . . .' And with that he threw the remains of the wet clay right into their faces.

'Bravo!' cried the princess. 'Well done. I would not have dared do that myself. You have won and *shall* be my husband!'

So Jack the Dunce married the princess and was crowned a king. Or so at any rate that was what it said in the papers.

Thumbelina

There was once a woman who wished for a very tiny child; but she did not know how or where to try and find one. So she went to an old witch and said:

'I do long for a little child! Can you help me to find one?'

'Oh, that can easily be arranged,' said the witch. 'Place this magic barleycorn in a flower pot, wait for a while and you shall see what you shall see.'

'Thank you,' said the woman, and she gave the witch a handful of silver.

She went straight home, planted the barleycorn and waited. Soon a great flower which looked like a tulip grew up; but the leaves were tightly closed, as if it were still a bud.

'What a beautiful flower!' said the woman, and she kissed its yellow and red petals. At once the flower opened with a pop and

there sat a tiny girl, delicate and graceful among the green foliage.

As she was barely a thumb's length in height, the woman called her Thumbelina. She made her a cradle out of a polished walnut shell, laid blue violet petals in it as a mattress and a rose petal for a quilt. Here Thumbelina slept at night, while in the daytime she played, rowing herself on a tulip petal boat with two white horsehairs as oars across a bowl of water. It was a lovely sight. Sometimes Thumbelina would sing in a voice so sweet and pure that everyone who heard it was enchanted by it. The woman came to love her dearly.

Then, alas, one night an ugly great toad came creeping through her window and saw the pretty little figure of Thumbelina lying asleep in the walnut shell.

'She would make a handsome wife for my son,' said the toad, and she picked up the shell and hopped with it down into the garden.

There, where the brook's edge was swampy and soft, the toad lived with her equally loathsome-looking son.

'Croak! croak! brek kek-kex!' was all he could say when he saw his graceful little bride.

'Sh! Don't speak so loud or you will wake her,' warned his mother. 'She might run away, for she is as light as swan's down. We will put her on one of the water lilies in the brook. It will be just like an island for her and she can't get away. We must go and get ready the state apartments where you and she will live together after the wedding.'

So it was that when Thumbelina awoke in the morning, she found herself quite cut off from land, surrounded on all sides by the green waters of the brook. She began to cry very bitterly, for there seemed no escape. The old toad arrived and, bowing low before her in the water, said:

'This is my son, your husband-to-be. You will live splendidly together in the marsh.'

'Croak! croak! brek kek-kex!' was all the son could say.

Then they carried off the walnut shell to install it in the state

bedchamber under the marsh, leaving Thumbelina to weep all alone on the lily leaf. But the fishes had heard all that had passed and, seeing the beautiful little maiden's distress, they assembled round her leaf.

'This must not be!' they cried. So they gnawed through the stalk of the water lily so that it floated away, bearing Thumbelina with it down the stream. The birds in the bushes sang beautifully for her and exclaimed, 'What a lovely little girl!'

A graceful little white butterfly fluttered round her and alighted on the leaf. This pleased Thumbelina, who by now

was feeling very happy, for it was so pleasant floating along on the glistening sun-drenched water. She took off her belt, tied one end of it gently round the butterfly and fastened the other to the leaf. Thus she travelled along even more swiftly, pulled by her elegant companion.

Suddenly a shadow passed over the sun and a huge maybug swooped down on Thumbelina and carried her away in his claws. The leaf was left still floating down the brook with the unfortunate butterfly helplessly fastened to it. Poor Thumbelina! She was terrified, and also miserable that the fine white butterfly could not free himself and would probably perish because of her.

Her captor placed her on a big green leaf and fed her on the sweet parts of flowers. He told her again and again how pretty she was. His fellow maybugs, however, did not agree:

'Why, she hasn't even got any feelers – how ugly she is!' they cried cruelly, until her admirer could bear it no longer and abandoned her to go where she pleased.

The whole summer long Thumbelina lived quite alone. She wove herself a bed out of blades of grass and hung it in the shelter of a great shamrock. She plucked honey out of the flowers for food and drank the dew which collected in them each morning. All too soon, however, the approach of winter brought an end to this happy existence. The wind blew cold and cruel and each snowflake seemed enormous to Thumbelina for she was only an inch high.

One day, when she was nearly frozen cold she stumbled on the

home of a field mouse. It was warm and comfortable, with a glorious larder of golden corn. The kind old field mouse welcomed Thumbelina and agreed to shelter her for the winter in return for a little housework and story-telling in the evenings.

A little later, the mouse's dearest friend, a rich old mole, came to call. As soon as he set eyes on the graceful figure of Thumbelina, he fell in love with her. The field mouse advised Thumbelina that this would be a very good match, but she did not like the mole, who hated the sunlight and the birds which she herself loved.

One day, as the three were strolling through one of the mole's corridors, they came upon a dead swallow. The mole and the field mouse ignored the poor creature, but, as soon as their backs were turned, Thumbelina stopped to embrace it. She found that it was not dead, but merely numbed with cold and exhaustion.

For many days Thumbelina crept out every night to nurse the swallow. Daily it grew in strength, until one day it announced that it was well enough to fly off and join its family in the warm countries. Would she not come with it? But Thumbelina knew that the field mouse would be very upset if she left her, so she sadly declined and said goodbye to the swallow with a heavy heart.

'Tweet-weet! Farewell, you good, pretty girl,' sang the swallow as it flew out into the sunshine.

All through the summer, the field mouse set Thumbelina to

194

work weaving and sewing her bridal clothes, for she had persuaded her that it was best to marry the old mole. Thumbelina was very unhappy. She could not bear the thought of living forever deep in the earth, far from the fresh air and the fragrance of flowers.

On the eve of her wedding, she left the house to say a last goodbye to all the beautiful creatures and plants in the fields above ground. Suddenly, 'Tweet-weet! tweet-weet!', a voice sounded just above her head. It was the swallow she had nursed back to health. She told him her sad plight and could not refrain from weeping.

'I am flying now far away to the warm countries,' said the swallow. 'Will you come with me? You can sit on my back and I will take you to a land where it is always summer and there are lovely flowers all the year round.'

'Yes, I will go with you!' cried Thumbelina, and she seated herself on the bird's back with her feet on the outspread wings and fastened her belt to one of his strongest feathers.

As the air grew colder high above the moun-tain ranges, she nestled more closely under the warmth of the bird's feathers, only peeping her little head out to admire all the wonders beneath her: vines hung with beautiful blue and green grapes, orange

and lemon trees delicately scenting the air and, at last, a palace of dazzling white marble with many swallows' nests resting on its lofty pillars.

'That is my home,' said the swallow; 'but it is not right that you live there. Choose yourself a flower from one of the splendid ones down there and I will put you safely into it.' And Thumbelina clapped her hands with joy and pleasure.

Then she pointed to where a great marble pillar lay broken in three pieces on the ground. Between these pieces grew the most beautiful tall lilies. The swallow flew down and set Thumbelina on one of their broad leaves. To her astonishment, there sat a little man as white and transparent as if he were made of glass. He wore a tiny golden crown on his head and dazzling wings on his shoulders. Thumbelina saw that he was no bigger than herself.

This was the angel of the flower. In each bloom lived just such a little man or woman, but this was the king of them all. When he saw Thumbelina the flower king was very glad, for she was the prettiest girl he had ever seen. So he asked her if she would become his wife and queen of all the flowers.

'But you shall no longer be called Thumbelina,' said the flower king. 'For that is an ugly name and you are far too lovely for it – we will call you Maia instead.' And they lived happily ever after.

The Princess and the Swineherd

There was once a prince who had fallen on hard times. His lands were quite small and poor, but he wanted very much to get married.

Now perhaps it was bold of him to ask the rich old emperor's daughter, but he loved her and, indeed, so handsome, brave and clever was he that there were hundreds of princesses who would have been glad to become his wife.

Although the prince could not afford to buy fine presents to send to the emperor's daughter, he did have a single beautiful rose which bloomed every fifth year on the grave of his father. Its perfume was so sweet that whoever smelt it forgot all sorrow and trouble. He also owned a nightingale which sang exquisitely. These he despatched to the princess in great silver boxes.

The emperor himself received the gifts and brought them to his daughter where she sat talking with her maids of honour. At the sight of the silver boxes she clapped her hands with joy:

'Presents!' she cried. 'Oh! I do hope it's a pussycat!'

But then out came the rose, brilliantly red and fragrant.

'Ugh, papa!' she cried, 'it is not artificial, it's a *natural* rose. How horrid!' And she stamped her little foot.

'Let's see what is in the second box before we get angry,' said the emperor.

When the nightingale emerged, it sang so beautifully that the whole court was spellbound. But the princess turned up her nose, saying:

'I can't bear birds in the house. I only like mechanical ones like the old musical box. Let the beastly thing fly away. I won't see the prince who sent these stupid gifts.'

When he heard this news, the prince was not dismayed. He stained his face brown, drew his hat down over his eyes and dressed himself in peasant clothes.

Then he went to the emperor and asked if he could work on his estate.

'Well,' said the emperor, 'as it happens, I do need a swineherd.

If you know anything about pigs you may have the job.'

So the handsome prince became the emperor's swineherd and went to live in a miserable dirty room down by the pigsty. All day long he sat and worked, and by the evening he had made a cooking pot. Attached to the pot were bells which, when it boiled, played a haunting lullaby. More clever by far, if you held your finger in the steam you could smell what everyone in the town was cooking for their supper.

The princess came by with her maids of honour and heard the pot playing a pretty tune. It was one she often played herself with one finger on the palace piano.

'He must be a very superior swineherd!' she exclaimed. 'Go and ask him the price of the instrument.'

But when one of the maids of honour returned with the answer, she blushed and giggled and would only whisper in the princess's ear:

'He says the price is ten kisses from you!'

The princess was shocked and angry, but the sound of the musical pot was so charming that eventually, she agreed, saying only to her maids of honour:

'You must stand close round me so that nobody can see.'

So the exchange took place; the princess came away with the pot, the swineherd received his kisses.

There was much laughter that night as the pot boiled and sang. All the ladies danced with pleasure, clapping their hands and crying:

'We know who will have soup and dumplings for supper and who will have bread pudding and cutlets; how fascinating!'

Next day the prince – that is, the swineherd – made a rattle which could play all the dance music that has ever been written.

When the princess saw this she demanded the price, but declared firmly that she would give no more kisses.

'A hundred kisses from the princess, or the rattle is not for sale,' came the reply.

'He must be mad!' exclaimed the princess. Then she thought perhaps he might accept just ten kisses from herself and the rest from her maids of honour.

But the swineherd refused to accept kisses from anyone but the princess, so, in the end, she allowed him to kiss her. But this time, the emperor caught sight of the crowd of giggling maids down by the pigsty. Rushing out in a fury, he was appalled by what met his gaze: the swineherd was in the act of taking his eighty-sixth kiss – from his own daughter!

'Be off and don't ever come back, you are both a disgrace!'

The princess and the swineherd were banished from his land.

'Oh, how unhappy I am. If only I had married the handsome prince!' wailed the princess.

Meanwhile, the swineherd went behind a tree, cleaned his face and changed into his fine princely clothes. Then he stood before the princess, who quickly curtsied before him.

'If only you had taken me then, indeed,' he said. 'But now I have seen your true nature. You rejected the simple gifts of an honest suitor, but for a mere trinket you kissed a filthy swineherd. You are not worthy to be my queen.'

He didn't listen to her cries of remorse but went on his way cheerfully, his proud head held high.

The Nightingale

A good many years ago, the emperor of China's palace was the most splendid in the world. It was made entirely of porcelain, exquisitely white and delicate. The garden was full of wonderful flowers decorated with silver bells so that no one should pass by without noticing them. Further on, the grounds stretched into a glorious forest of high trees right down to the sea. In these trees lived a nightingale which sang so beautifully that poor fishermen tending their nets stood still and listened in wonder.

One day the emperor was reading one of the books which praised his city, his palace and his garden. Suddenly he saw the words, 'The nightingale that sings in his grounds is the most exquisite in the whole world.'

Neither the emperor nor any of his court had ever heard of the nightingale. Immediately the search was begun for the bird which was the jewel of the kingdom. Courtiers ran up and down all the staircases, and through all the halls and corridors. No one could give a clue as to the whereabouts of the nightingale until at last they came to the kitchen. There was a poor little girl who was cleaning dishes.

'The nightingale?' she said. 'I know it well; yes, it sings gloriously. Every evening when I rest in the forest on my way home I listen to him and he comforts and cheers me.'

The girl agreed to conduct the chief courtier to the place in the wood where the nightingale usually sang. When they were half way there, a cow began to low.

'Ah, there it is!' cried the grand gentleman. 'What a miraculous sound for so small a creature.'

'No, that is just a cow lowing,' said the kitchen girl. 'We have a long way to go yet.'

Then some frogs started croaking in the marsh.

'Glorious!' cried the chief courtier. 'Now I hear it – it sounds just like church bells.'

'No, those are only frogs,' said the girl. 'But it will not be long now.'

And finally they came to where the nightingale nested.

'That's his nest. Look, there he is . . .' said the kitchen girl.

And she pointed to a small dull-coloured bird high up in a tree.

The chief courtier was astonished. It was so small and looked so ordinary.

'Little nightingale,' called the kitchen girl, 'our gracious emperor wishes you to sing before him.'

The nightingale agreed with pleasure and followed them to the

court, where the emperor and all his courtiers were waiting.

When they arrived, the whole palace was gaily decorated in preparation. Thousands of golden lamps gleamed in the great porcelain halls, while glorious flowers adorned every table. There was a tremendous bustle of excitement and activity.

The emperor sat waiting on his throne in the great hall. Near him stood a golden perch on which the nightingale was to sit. Everyone was dressed in his finest clothes and all looked doubtfully at the drab little bird as it prepared to sing.

The song was so magnificent, its melody so sweet and clear that the tears ran down the emperor's cheeks, for the music had

touched his heart. His courtiers too were quite entranced.

The nightingale was such a success that the emperor demanded it remain at court. A delicate silver cage was built and twelve servants were chosen for the task of taking the bird out for an airing twice a day. Each held tightly to a silken thread fastened to the nightingale's leg. The poor wild creature got no enjoyment from its daily tastes of freedom. But it continued to sing with gentle good will, for it loved nothing better than to give happiness.

Then one day a parcel arrived for the emperor from the emperor of Japan. It was labelled 'The Nightingale' and inside was a clockwork bird, brilliantly ornamented with diamonds, rubies and sapphires. When it was wound up, it sang a beautiful waltz, moving its shining tail up and down in time to the music. The emperor and his court were overjoyed!

'Now the two birds must sing a duet together,' declared the emperor.

But the duet was not a success, for the real nightingale sang in its own natural way, while the artificial bird sang its familiar waltz tune. So the clockwork bird sang alone. It sang perfectly – the same piece thirty-three times over, and still it was not tired.

217

Marvellous! And it was so much prettier than the first nightingale.

While the emperor and his court were occupied admiring the artificial bird, the nightingale managed to escape from its perch and flew back to the forest.

Everyone declared it was an ungrateful creature to behave thus and the emperor was so annoyed that he banished the nightingale from his kingdom. Soon all this was forgotten in the popularity of the new bird. It stood permanently on a silken cushion at the emperor's side, surrounded by sumptuous gifts. It was given the title 'High Imperial After-Dinner Singer' and several learned books were written about it.

A year went by. Then one evening, when the clockwork bird was in full voice and the emperor lay in bed listening contentedly, there was a loud 'whizz! crack!', a slow whirring, and the music stopped and the bird became motionless and silent.

The emperor leapt out of bed. He summoned the doctor – but what could *he* do? Even the imperial watchmaker could only restore the bird to a feeble state of health. It would be able to sing once a year only from now on, or he could not answer for the consequences.

A sadness fell over the whole kingdom. The emperor seemed suddenly to age without the comfort of his clockwork musician.

After five years, the emperor was very ill indeed and seemed certain to die. A new emperor was chosen and the people stood in the streets awaiting the news of their ruler's death.

Cold and pale, the emperor lay in his bed. High up, above him, the window was open and the moon shone on the dying man and the artificial bird.

When the emperor opened his eyes, he saw the figure of Death standing over him.

Then from the window, suddenly, came the most wonderful song. It was the little nightingale, who had heard of the emperor's sad plight and come to sing to him to bring him comfort and hope. As it sang, the figure of Death grew fainter and fainter, until it vanished clean away. The blood began to flow more quickly in the emperor's veins and the colour returned to his cheeks.

'Sleep and grow strong again,' said the nightingale. 'I will sing you a lullaby.'

He sang and the emperor fell into a deep and refreshing slumber from which he awoke in the morning fully recovered. The nightingale was still singing in the window when his servants came and found the emperor miraculously cured.

The nightingale was hailed as the saviour of the nation. The emperor was going to throw the clockwork bird away, but the live bird stopped him.

'No. Keep it as you have done till now: it served you well as long as it could. No one can do more.'

The emperor agreed, and the little nightingale flew back to its nest in the forest, promising to return when he wanted to or when the emperor was in any trouble or distress.

The Garden of Paradise

Once upon a time there was a king's son who preferred listening to the stories his grandmother told him to doing his lessons. Of all the stories his favourite was that of the Garden of Paradise.

'In this garden,' his grandmother would say, 'Adam and Eve, the first couple, lived. Every flower there is a delicious cake. Just one bite from such a cake and you learn a new lesson: geography, history or tables.'

Years passed and by the time the prince was seventeen he had acquired many beautiful books from every corner of the earth. He read of the people and customs of many lands, but nowhere could he find any information about the Garden of Paradise whose secrets he so longed to learn.

One day, as he was walking alone in the wood, a great storm blew up. The sky grew as black as night and the rain came down in torrents. Slipping and stumbling blindly through the downpour, the drenched prince saw before him a great cave brightly lit by a

huge roaring fire. Over it a large, ugly old woman was roasting a whole deer.

'Come closer; sit by the fire and dry your clothes,' she said. 'Welcome to the Cave of the Four Winds. My sons will be here soon.'

'Thank you, but who are your sons?' asked the prince.

'They are the four winds of the world, and a more mischievous bunch of good-for-nothings you'd have difficulty finding. But I make them behave. Just let one of them step out of line and – before you know it in he goes, straight into one of those sacks you see hanging there. But here comes one of them now. You shall see for yourself.'

With a rush of piercing cold air the North Wind appeared. He was dressed in bear skins, long icicles hung in his beard and hail-stones fell from him as he moved.

'Good morning, Mother. I have just returned from the icy polar sea, where I have been pursuing the bear and walrus hunters. Just